THEY DON'T RUN RED TRAINS ANYMORE

HEIDI VON PALLESKE

SMART HOUSE BOOKS

Heidi von Palleske/Smart House Books
Toronto, On.
www.smarthousebooks.com

Publisher's Note: This is a work of fiction. Names, characters, places, and incidents are a product of the author's imagination. Locales and public names are sometimes used for atmospheric purposes. Any resemblance to actual people, living or dead, or to businesses, companies, events, institutions, or locales is completely coincidental.

Book Layout © 2017 Smart House Books
Cover art, John Nobrega, *St. Lucy,* oil on canvas, 1997, Toronto, On.
Cover Design, Aaron Rachel Brown, 2017

Printed in Canada on recycled paper
Printing Icon
1305 Morningside Ave, #15
Toronto, On., M1B 4Z5

ISBN 978-0-9689718-3-3

TORONTO ARTS COUNCIL

FUNDED BY THE CITY OF TORONTO

ONTARIO ARTS COUNCIL
CONSEIL DES ARTS DE L'ONTARIO
an Ontario government agency
un organisme du gouvernement de l'Ontario

To Cavanagh Matmor

and

in memory of
Mary Hecht

"An act such as this is prepared within the silence of the heart;
as is a great work of art."

—ALBERT CAMUS

CHAPTER 1

I was once at a subway station when somebody chose to jump.
I remember the screech of the brakes, a dull thump and blood.
Blood all over. It was rush hour and across town commuters
complained about the inconvenience of this eight o'clock
jump. It was actually five minutes past. I focussed on the large
digital clock. The display in red.

An hour later I was seated in my life drawing class, gripping
the edge of a worktable. A man's voice asking, "Hey, are you
okay?"

"Fine," I say, "I'm fine."

I had been fine. Fine enough to redirect myself onto an
alternative route. Up the escalator, away from the southbound
train and over to the east-west line. West two stops, then a
streetcar down Spadina until the familiar Dundas intersection.
From there I walked past the Art Gallery with its Henry
Moore sprawled lazily on the concrete entranceway. My
footsteps fell quickly on the pavement until I arrived at the
Ontario School of Art. Only fifteen minutes late for my first
class of the day. Safe in the security of routine.

I take a seat, open my sketchbook, and smooth a fresh page
with my hand. I busy myself, sorting my charcoals and pencils,
concentrating on the present. On the task of putting an image
to paper.

"We will be working with a live model again today. Last
week we did a series of quick sketches, capturing movement
and shape. This week I am looking for something more
detailed," my teacher's voice instructs as he opens the
classroom door.

She walks into my life drawing class, a study in vulnerable bravado. She drops her robe. But I can't take my eyes from the face. Quiet and trusting. A green unfocused gaze. Long, black tresses. A velvet curtain veiling her shoulders, her back, her breasts. I glance to see if she is naturally dark. She catches me and smiles.

The charcoal is heavy in my hand. Uncooperative. I imagine laying tracing paper over her to copy the lines of her body. Stretch her like a canvas, and rub soft graphite over her curves. But then she's off the stool, leaning forward. Head dropped, hair flowing about her like a troubled ocean. I grip the charcoal firmly, attack the paper. Clear my mind from the morning's upset. If I can capture her life then maybe I will wash the other image away.

Finally she raises her head, adjusts her body then drapes her robe loosely over slight, soft shoulders. As she breezes past me, I become aware of her skin. Of the soft burnt terra-cotta of her flesh. Alive and warm and unlike any shade I've ever seen on any nude model before.

"Is that supposed to be me?" she laughs, pointing at my easel's offering.

Humiliated, I close my sketch pad and mutter something about how difficult she is to translate into two dimensions. A gentle shrug and her robe slackens to reveal a momentary flash of her three dimensions. I feel the rush of blood in my cheeks and I know that my fair colouring is betraying me. She laughs again, without embarrassment. Then she simply walks away.

Good-bye. There is nothing as attractive as a woman who is leaving.

Life drawing had never been my first love. But I didn't miss a class after that day, always hoping for her return. My professor misunderstood my dedication and offered me extra tutelage after class. I explained that my heart was in sculpting, that I was only taking life drawing because it was mandatory, that there was no chance I would ever improve. But Boris was not one to take no for an answer.

"If you trust me, you will improve."

We were lovers briefly. I didn't improve.

*****

Lying beside Boris in bed, thinking about soft, dark tresses. He shifts to get up and I ask him about her.

"Who?"

"The model. You know, the beautiful one."

"Oh please Alex, I teach how many classes a week? You can't expect me to remember each and every model."

"She wasn't fat. She was different. Exotic."

"Every woman is exotic when she has her clothes off," he laughs.

"She had dark hair and green eyes. She could be Persian or Middle Eastern."

"Ah."

"Ah?"

"Premika. She's from Montreal. She moved here last year. God knows why."

"She's French-Canadian then?"

"Only in her pretensions." Boris has a slightly bored tone to his voice. "Her father was East Indian. Her mother had an affair when they were both at McGill. He went back to India before Premika was born."

Boris has had enough. He puts a finger to my lips to quiet me, "Alex, please, she's a model. Pretty, yes. But nothing beyond that."

He moves to get up and reaches for his clothes. I turn away from him and stare out the window as he dresses. I love windows. Love how something so transparent can fit into a solid, opaque structure. *Fenestration*: The arrangement of windows in a building. They offer the promise of freedom. School I remember as simply one classroom window after another. Staring beyond the fingerprints I'd place myself outside, away from the squeaking chalk, the squeaking chairs and the endless squeaking of the teacher's repetitive voice.

"Why sculpture?" Boris asks me and his voice brings me back into his room, away from the memories of past windows. He is standing above me, buttoning his last few buttons, arranging his appearance. He is neither bohemian nor neat. He could be described as acceptable if it wasn't for his carefully contrived, casual air. His hair is perfectly combed then tousled with deliberate strokes. The tie is tied properly then loosened a bit at the neck. The shirt is tucked evenly into pressed trousers but an oversized, slightly creased, linen jacket is thrown on top. And above the costume he wears an expression. What is it? Amusement? Exasperation?

I'm suddenly shy. Dressed, he is once again the teacher and I, his pupil. It doesn't matter that we were, just moments ago, the beast with two backs; he is now dressed and I am not. I pull the sheets over my damp body. The tops of my thighs still sticky with him. I want to shower but I'm afraid of insulting him.

"Sculpture is poetry in form," I tell him.

He sits on the edge of the bed. Pulls the sheet from my body and cups my breast in his hand. His thumb and forefinger close in on my nipple.

"Poetry isn't relevant. Who sits down and cries over a poem by Donne, Milton or Wordsworth?"

His thumb and forefinger press just a little harder, squeezing my nipple between them. He wants a reaction. I give him no more than a wince.

"Wordsworth was crap when it was written."

"Most popular poet of his time," he corrects me.

"Not more popular than Byron."

He shrugs in dismissal. "It doesn't matter. No one cares about poetry today. It's a thing of the past. Like the sculpture you love so much. It has no currency. Only academics and hangers-on bother about it. And *that* is the point."

"Well, *we're* discussing it," I argue, "so it can't be that irrelevant."

"You, my dear, are a hanger-on. Your interests are outdated, old and irrelevant."

"They must be. I'm sleeping with *you.*"

One last quick pinch of his finger and thumb before releasing my chastised nipple.

"Get dressed," he orders. "I have a class in half an hour."

I reach for my panties and undershirt. I pull the cotton shirt on first.

"You're too much of a romantic," he tells me. "You'll never survive the art world."

I slip into the panties, facing the window as I dress. The German word for window is *fenster*. The French word is *fenêtre*. To throw oneself out of a window is *defenestration*. In order to guarantee success a minimum height of five stories must be employed. Anything less will fall short, so to speak.

"Art," he lectures, "is living. It is not what you see in those mausoleums you call museums. It has purpose. Life. It is not bourgeois decoration. The sooner you learn that, the more successful you will be."

"You can hardly call Michelangelo bourgeois." I fasten my jeans and reach for my belt.

"It's been done. Why repeat it? If you have the audacity to challenge Michelangelo's work, you better be up for the task. You might be a good sculptor, you may even be the best in your class, but you're no Michelangelo. You don't work in stone. And trust me, neither wax nor clay have staying power. You know, you might consider concrete if you want something current and weighty."

"I can make bronzes from my waxes and clay…"

"Expensive."

"Well, what do you suggest?"

"Concrete installations. Something edgier. You have to change your focus or you'll never carve out a name for yourself. You won't amount to anything if you follow in someone else's footsteps."

My third grade teacher also told me that I would never amount to anything, but she said it was because I wasn't a team player. I was too much of a dreamer, always staring out windows. I wasn't dreaming though; I was studying. Watching how the quality of light changed throughout the day. Measuring the shadows as they fell across the playground, changing shape and direction as the day wore on. Keeping my eye trained on a point in the distance. Monitoring that solitary spot on the horizon where all things seem to emanate and return when you draw an imaginary line from all that is close and tangible to beyond where the eye can see. I wasn't a dreamer; I was an explorer. An explorer in search of infinity.

My present teacher, Boris, touches my shoulder. It's time to leave.

"Think about what I said. Don't let your ego get in the way of your talent."

I gather my things and, with my knapsack flung over my shoulder, head for the door. Boris lies, fully dressed and stretched across the bed, watching me. I turn back to him to ask him more about Premika but he shakes his head and, with a shooing hand-gesture, sends me on my way.

*****

I reworked that sketch of her, *Premika*, many times. Why? No one would ever see it; it would never be displayed or viewed. It was an exercise. Something to attempt and then throw away. But I couldn't. I knew it was lacking; I hadn't gotten it quite right.

"I don't know why it bothers you so much," says Boris as he lifts his shrimp dumpling out of its bamboo steamer. Even the most slippery noodle will not escape the grip of his chopsticks.

"Maybe you just need more practice."

"I can't afford to hire models," I tell him flatly. I put down my chopsticks and reach for the fork. No point in embarrassing myself with a dumpling dropped in my lap.

"You should do what I did when I was in art school. Go to strip clubs."

I stare across the table at him, incredulous. Boris points at a small plate of ribs. I shake my head and he finishes them off.

"I'm not you."

"What is that supposed to mean?"

"Just that it may be more difficult for a female student to pick up models in strip clubs than it might be for a young male student."

"Oh, I see. Well go along with some of the male students then."

"I don't think it'll work for me."

"Of course it will. It's like this. They'll see you sketching them at a club. Go to The Brass Rail. It's cheap there and they don't mind if you nurse a beer all night. Anyhow, one of the girls will invariably come over to see what you're doing. *Especially* since you are a woman. Now, you may not be the greatest artist in the world, but you're the best she'll ever see. By the end of the night she'll agree to pose."

"Do I pay her?"

"Never."

"Why would she agree then?" I ask.

Boris shrugs. "A chance for someone to view her in a different light perhaps. A chance to be seen as more than she is. Or maybe, a chance to be seen for the best she could possibly be. It's a way for her to escape her reality."

"No," I say, "I don't buy that."

"Okay," he laughs, "it's the hope you can immortalize her. Promise a woman immortality and she'll offer up her soul."

I wonder if thousands of women have posed for artists as much for their own satisfaction as the artists'? Does a mistress sit for her painter-lover to please him or does she choose a painter for a lover so that she can sit for him?

"Did you ever sleep with them?"

"With whom?"

"The strippers you used as models?"

"Well, there were a few I would've slept with, but by the time I finished painting them I'd lost my interest. Staring at a naked woman for six hours at a go kills all sense of mystery I suppose."

"That's because you objectify women."

"Not women, *models*. There's a difference. Come on, don't be all feminist and touchy about this. Rotten fruit doesn't complain to the still-life artist that it's being objectified, does it?"

"Rotten fruit *is* an object; it's entirely different. You have a naked body in a room with you. Your model moves and poses exactly as you say. You must find some temptation in that power. A model yielding to your every command."

Boris laughs. There is affection in it, but it comes with implied hierarchy. In time this will change. One day I will no longer be his student. I will move on and he will find someone else to mentor.

"That's just silly and romantic." He waves to the waitress, using that international sign that signals that she should bring the bill.

"Really? Because I remember you saying that you *preferred* women with their clothes off," I remind him.

"I suppose you're right. But at some point a difficult decision must be made. Do I want to fuck her or draw her?"

"Never both?"

"Rarely," he says in a very urbane manner. "As an artist you must distance yourself, otherwise you cannot be objective and your art becomes a lie. Love, on the other hand, is capricious at best." He smiles. "Remind me never to paint you."

We left the restaurant. Boris went across the street to the Art College and I went home to redraw Premika from memory. No nude model before me. No nuance or personality to distract me. I worked at it. Distancing myself. Detached from her and anything she might have inspired in me that morning we met. At last the likeness was good but the sketch evoked no emotional reaction. The drawing said nothing about the subject. Nothing more than the shape of her body and the tilt of her head. I wasn't Boris. I wasn't cut out for sketching. It's too quick. A *catch and release* style of art.

I put the sketch, and all thoughts of her, away. I finished the term. Passed my life drawing class and, with all my requisite credits completed, I graduated from art college. I could, at last, concentrate solely on my sculpting.

CHAPTER 2

I'm standing on a platform below the city's surface. There is a rumble of thunder deep in the tunnel, announcing an approaching train. Commuters shift and jockey for position. I ape their posture, moving my weight from foot to foot as I stare across the tracks. They do not know my discomfort. They do not see the fine stone dust that has settled between my clothes and my skin. I do not scratch. I do not pull at my neckline. I look like them. I blend.

I stare down at the tracks. Mice run about in the darkness. They know when to make their move. When to run for safety. They too have adapted.

I shift my stare across the tracks and focus on the billboards. Stylish friends laugh it up as they all drink the same beer. Not a wine drinker amongst them. They are beautiful looking, with straight teeth, shiny hair and sexy clothes. They are full of joy, of life. Beside the beer party poster is a more sobering message. White letters on a black background tell you whom to call if you are suffering, or if you know of someone suffering, from domestic violence. The abused woman could be your sister, your daughter, a friend. Hey, it might even be one of the happy people from the beer ad! But it is the third poster that captures my attention. The third poster stops me in my tracks. It seems that Venus herself stands on a huge oyster shell, a red sash draped about her, concealing little. Her nipples, her pelvis, barely hidden from public view. The red stands in contrast to the turquoise ocean surrounding her, its waves licking at her thighs. And in her outstretched hand rests what? A bottle of *Infinity*. The symbol, that sideways letter 8, underlining its name. It's the newest, sexiest perfume to hit the market. Or so the caption reads.

Suddenly the image is blurred by a train. People push past me, cramming themselves inside. I wait for the commotion to pass, for the train to depart, and steal back to the billboard.

There's no mistaking her. Same veil of dark hair, same smooth brow, same green eyes and adamant lips. There she is in technicolor. Two dimensions and two tracks away, unmoving, until another train disrupts my view.

I leave her, get on the train, and grab onto a pole near the door. Only now, surrounded by the rush hour commuters do I acknowledge my skin's irritation. Wherever my clothes touch my body I itch. The subway car is crowded and close. The artificial heating intensifies my discomfort. At my waistline, under my bra, even inside my panties, the stone dust making its way into my skin. I pull the cloth away from my body and hope that nobody sees me. It's the same every night. My day job, designing and cutting headstones, makes me very uncomfortable. Stone cutting is tedious and messy. The fine dust travels on air and permeates clothes. I itch everywhere from the grinding of stone. I will myself not to scratch, to appear composed and comfortable. Nobody detects my silent discomfort. Not the business woman across from me who sits reading her journal, not the students laughing at a shared joke, and not the billboard of Premika with her bottle of *Infinity*.

*****

The envelope sat out from the usual bills and fliers. Ivory vellum and hand addressed in broad, secure lettering. Fountain pen. The return address was for a gallery on Bathurst Street. *The Cutting Edge*. Could just as easily have been a hair salon as a gallery. I put the envelope on my kitchen table. It could wait until after the much anticipated relief of my evening shower.

If only I worked alone when I cut stone, I'd strip myself bare then hose myself down at day's end.

The water runs over my head and down my shoulders. Rivers fall across my breasts and belly. I lather soap under my armpits and into my pubic hair until every itch is satisfied, every irritation eliminated. My skin is restored, refreshed. But my muscles still ache beyond reason.

I should appreciate my job more. A degree in fine art does not qualify one for many jobs. Others from my graduating class have gone on to acquire teaching degrees or pursued work in advertising or design. Although I can draw, my ability as a sculptor outweighs that as an illustrator or designer. And so it is Milestone Memorial for me, working for Amadeo, an eccentric task master. I found the job through my friend Jack. Jack had graduated from art school a few years before me. He didn't want to work in advertising or to continue his schooling to become a teacher and so, when he read an ad for a small company that makes headstones, he responded. Jack had been working there for a few years, designing the stencils and cutting the words into the granite, when Amadeo's nephew decided to go back to Italy. Amadeo was in need of some cheap labour. At first he didn't want to hire me. Said that it was no place for a girl to work. But after a conversation about sculpture and stone, the job was mine. Jack showed me what was required and helped me with the heavier work until I was grinding and cutting and polishing like an old pro. Amadeo saw a future for me but I assured him that I was only working until I could establish myself as an artist. He shook his head. Almost two years later and I am still grinding, cutting and polishing.

My evening shower complete, I slip into a clean cotton work shirt and fresh panties. I relight the pilot on my stove and put the kettle on for some hot tea. Then I open the envelope. An invitation from Boris.

*****

"Still drawing?"

At last...

At first I was surprised to see her at Boris's opening. She swept into the gallery and embraced my ex-teacher with all the intimacy of an old friend. Ah, of course! She must have been his lover as well. He probably seduced her the very day I had sketched her. I had taken a drawing of her home. He had taken *her*. Boris was not one to miss an opportunity. I wonder how long their affair lasted. Whether we had shared him for a time. I got an undeserved B+ out of my affair with him. I wonder what she got.

"Yes," I say, "I'm still drawing, sometimes. Premika, right?"

"I didn't think you'd remember me." She smiles. We both see the lie.

"How could I forget you? You laughed at my work."

"Did I?" she laughs and turns to go. My god, she is Zephyrus, the west wind. Breeze through here, breeze through there. Cause a little disturbance and then just blow away. Lightly touching, never settling.

She turns to go, to turn me into a memory. But Boris saves the day. He intercepts, two glasses of champagne in his hands. One for each of us.

"This is the real art of today. It challenges. It objects. Art objects. You get it? *Objets d'art*. Art objects!" Boris smiles at his own cleverness. "I have a mixed media installation in the next room. Have you seen it yet?"

She shakes her head no.

"Well I think you might find it interesting. You'll want to see it before I start my speech."

Premika and I enter the adjoining room where Boris has his installation. A large canvas displays Premika; a nude in oil. It's not bad. Certainly recognizable. What Boris lacks in his ability to create flesh - flesh that seems alive - he makes up for in line and grace. I hate admitting that Boris has an elegance when he puts his hand to the female form. It is hard to judge the painting, however, because every few seconds an image is projected over various parts of her body, obliterating my view. Images of starving children flash across her breasts. A war wages on her mound of Venus. Corporate images flash across her thighs, her belly, and arms.

I look at the woman who posed for the work. Watch her face as the images continue their assault on her body. Premika stands frozen. Her face, a mask that hides her disappointment. Suddenly the gallery seems quiet but for the timed click of the projector changing slides overhead, and the in and out sound of Premika's breath. We are alone now. The other guests are in the main room. I hear the familiar clearing of throats and hushing that comes before a speech. But Premika makes no move and so I stay with her, watching as the projected images rape Premika's perfect, naked form. Listening to the perpetrator's distant voice.

"First of all, I'd like to thank you all for coming. Of course I'm sure you've all had enough wine and hors d'oeuvres to make it worth your while," Boris pauses for the polite laughter. "The Cutting Edge Gallery promises to be the most exciting art movement to hit this city. Art has to live. Just as religion must evolve and change to suit a society's needs, so must art evolve and change in order to reflect a society."

I can hear murmurs of approval. The audience, no doubt, consists primarily of his chosen artists and students, their families and their friends.

"Is your work displayed tonight?" Premika asks me quietly.

"No."

"Why not?"

"I didn't want to show in this venue," I lie. I don't want her to know that Boris doesn't think that my work holds currency.

She nods slowly and turns her gaze back to Boris's oil of her. He has let her down. He has used her body as a map to display the horrors and inequities of the world. Her body, on canvas, *is* no more than a backdrop for his politics. But to Premika, all it says is that her beauty didn't deserve a display of its own.

"Beneath the silly slide show, the painting does have merit," I tell her.

"Do you really think so?"

"It has grace. The flesh is a bit uninspired but that has never been a strong point for Boris. He's an illustrator not a colourist. Besides, your skin would be very difficult to duplicate."

"I wouldn't know."

I walk over to the projector's mount. Feel along the wall behind it and pull the plug from the socket. The machine's clicking stops, the images cease and Premika's body is free of the woes of the world.

His painting is suggestive enough. Lovely even. She looks to be sleeping. Head thrown back, her dark hair cascading down, almost touching the ground. The breasts are certainly hers; one arm rests between them. Thighs slightly parted. Long, tight paths that almost invite the eye to swoop over the flesh and experience it. Almost. Almost. But the flesh doesn't beg that you touch it. The pose is as strong as a Schiele or a Klimt but the flesh is weak. Why?

"It has a Klimt-esque quality," I offer.

"Klimt?"

"Austrian painter, famous for…"

"Yes, I know who Klimt is," she cuts me off. And just when I think she will mention *The Kiss,* that overproduced image that hangs in every hip young woman's bedroom, she surprises me with, "he used his talent to fuck pretty, young women. A bit like someone we both know. He, too, liked redheads," she says pointedly, gesturing to my red hair.

"Yes," I reply, "it was rumored that Klimt's red-haired model committed suicide when he became bored with her. Both as a model and as a mistress."

"Well don't despair. No one would ever kill herself over Boris!" She laughs. We know each other's secret.

In the next room Boris, the shared man, continues, "Art is not decoration. Beauty is an artificial construct…"

But the woman beside me *is* beautiful. Her veins course with blood, her lungs fill with air. She sweats, she cries, she lives. Her beauty is not an artificial construct.

"I could immortalize you," I whisper.

She stands still for what seems a very long time. The speeches have stopped in the next room. The din of an eating, drinking, talking crowd is just a backdrop to her silence. An inhale of breath. A decision.

"Shall we go?" She suggests and I know I've triumphed over every criticism Boris has ever cast my way.

He is chatting with another art school graduate. I should say hello but I pass by them. Premika in hand. He pauses. He doesn't seem unhappy or surprised. Just passed over.

*****

She was too impatient for a taxi, too cold to walk, so we stood, waiting for the inevitability of a subway train. A red one.

"I hate the silver ones. I'm not sure why."

"Perhaps because they have no sense of a past. No history," I suggest.

"No," she replies flatly, "I think it's because they're ugly."

And so we let five of them pass, waiting for a red subway train.

"So how would you paint me?" she asks.

"I wouldn't. I'd sculpt you."

"Would you make me beautiful?"

"Of course. Art is truthful."

"The truth isn't necessarily beautiful."

"No. But you are," I say. "If I'm to be truthful, I'd have to sculpt you as you are. Look, Boris is full of shit. He claims to deny beauty because he believes that political art is the only art worth doing. Everything else is bourgeois. But it's a fad, about as important as bell-bottoms or Mohawks. Besides, if he really believed that beauty is irrelevant then why does he seduce so many beautiful women? He can't help himself. He's attracted to beauty."

Another silver train passes us by.

"Are you attracted to beauty?"

"Who isn't?"

Premika shifts her weight. Looks across the tracks and sees herself displayed on the perfume billboard.

"I'm not," she says as she steps toward me.

I feel the breeze of an approaching train but I don't turn to see what colour it might be. Premika breathes and her sweetened exhale touches my cheek.

"I'm attracted to talent," she whispers. Her hand lifts my chin. And then her lips almost brush mine. And she stays close, inhaling my very breath, taking a part of my soul into her lungs. Then her mouth presses against mine. My eyes close. Somewhere I still hear the sound of an approaching train. Please let it be silver. I yield to the soft touch of her femininity, lost on the platform, greedy to hold onto the moment. But then she's gone. The doors close and a red train speeds away.

*****

I wake at the crack of noon or shortly thereafter. Mustn't get up too quickly, bump my head. I throw my leg over the side of the bed; my foot touches the cold hardwood floor. A stiff and constant breeze is entering through the open window. That last tease of Indian summer is over. I can either brace myself for the shock and close the window or I can draw my foot back under the covers and deny the change of season.

The phone rings. I consider letting the answering machine pick it up. But it could be her. I slam down the window and pick up on the fourth ring.

"Hello?"

There is a pause. The line is open, but no one responds at first.

"Hello?" I repeat myself. My voice has a croaky, sleepy sound.

"Hello." It's Boris, calling to check in, or rather check up on me. "You left in a hurry."

"I was tired. But I did see everything, Boris."

"Oh? And what did you think?"

What does it matter? Why should my opinion mean anything to him? He has his dogma; he doesn't need my approval or thoughts.

"Are you angry with me?" he asks.

I have to pee. That first, demanding pee of the morning. If I beg off the phone immediately Boris will assume that I am angry, miffed that he didn't choose to show any of my work. I cross my legs.

"Should I be angry?" I answer with a question.

"No," his words are well chosen now. "We parted company. Our affair ended and so we don't owe anything to each other. Do we?"

"Boris," I say, "even if we were still fucking each other from time to time, I wouldn't expect that you would display my work. We have different approaches. Let's leave it at that."

I really have to pee now. A burning sensation is shooting up inside of me.

"I would show your work," he tells me, "if you could come up with something that fits our mandate..."

"I can do better than that," I cut him off. "I won't create something to fit your mandate but rather to answer your mandate. Now I really must go."

Relief. Except that now the glove has been thrown down.

CHAPTER 3

The morning crowd stares ahead. Waits for a train that will take them to their work. It is a five day a week routine. Day in and day out drudgery. It wears them down. It wears us all down. We are a worn down society. The daily grind has ground us into dry powder, incapable of original thought, unable to feel, too tired to create. We blow from appointment to appointment, filling ourselves with things.

I wait with them because of my lack of success. When the train arrives I slip inside, reminding myself that this is only my corporeal being. There is more. There are dreams. There are desires.

The doors close. I lean against a pole, check my reflection in the glass. Am I becoming part of working society simply because I follow this morning ritual? I may have my other world, my real work, but the reality is that to live one must make a living. I make my living from people dying.

Milestone Memorials. This is my job, I remind myself again. Not my work. Still, I can't help but leave my mark from time to time. Create a little beauty on the plain, cold granite. But I'm fooling myself. Carving in stone isn't what it was once cracked up to be. We might work in stone -- grey, cold granite -- but what were once hammers and chisels are now sand-blasters, grinding machines, drills and polishers. Designs are drawn and cut out on stencils. The lettering is done on templates. How is that a worthy use of stone?

I take up my place, begin. I replace the nozzle on my sandblaster and change the pressure from 100 pounds to ten. I move in, study the markings of a Stansteal grey granite stone. Is the pattern tight in the granite? Are the flecks and veins close together? Such markings deserve special attention. I just can't help myself. I sneak in a small detail, adding a griffin for the lawyer, a caduceus for the doctor and roses for those who are young. I remove the sacred stencil to add some truly original detail. I try, really try, to personalize the dead.

"Just give them the basics. That's all they want." Jack tells me. Again.

"What's wrong with a little beauty Jack?"

"Oh for Chrissake, it's only a marker. It ain't art!"

It ain't art. I can console myself that my days here are not as long as Jack's. I can go home, find some energy to create something of my own imagination. But Jack has become invaluable. To both Amadeo and to me.

I met Jack in my first year of art school. He was unlike the other students. Rougher, perhaps. Coming from the working class he was, in many ways, a dose of pragmatism in an idealistic, cloistered school. He was attractive, manly and outspoken. He was also a man in possession of a kiln, willing to fire up pieces for a small fee. Not only did Jack fire my work in his kiln, he also helped with my glazes. And through the process he became my most trusted friend.

Although Jack attended art school he was, for the most part, self-taught. He came from a long line of Scottish stone masons and had learned to build a dry stone wall by the time he was ten. He understood stone, it was his birth-right, and so working at Amadeo's Milestone Memorials was an obvious fit. Our boss, Amadeo, relied on Jack for choosing and negotiating the deal on the granite and, on rare occasions, the marble used for his headstones.

"That reminds me, Amadeo wants to see you before you go home today."

"What about?"

Jack shrugs. "Maybe it's about all the extras you keep etching into the stones. The customers aren't paying for that, you know. Your extra time costs him money."

"Maybe," I say doubtfully. I know that the extras have been good for business.

"Maybe it's 'cause you keep coming in late."

"Probably."

I put on protective glasses, lift my sandblaster, get to work. Jack continues with his stencils while I work. It is only when he stops for coffee that he interrupts me, stopping the noise of machinery.

"Did you hear about the guy on Bay Street? Leaned against a window on the twenty-somethingth floor of an office tower and by fluke the glass cracks and he crashes down to his death. His last words were, 'Hey, watch this!' "

"It's an urban myth," I tell him.

"Nope. A friend of mine read it in the paper."

"Right. It happened in New York last year and Chicago the year before that..."

"Really?"

It amazes me that someone as cynical as Jack can also be so naive.

"They say it was an accident."

There is a term for that. Death by misadventure. A car drives too fast. A parachute doesn't open. A man throws himself onto a window just for laughs.

"If it did happen, and it probably didn't, it wasn't an accident. It was suicide, Jack. And the family is just covering it up."

Jack thinks for a moment. We've both witnessed the deception: suicides disguised as accidents, weeping families not so lost in grief that they haven't the wit to concoct a lie and, with the grinding of stone, we collaborate each story by etching the word *beloved* before the names. I have no idea how many headstones I've engraved for suicides. In truth, not even statisticians can be sure of the numbers because any cause of death is preferable to a self inflicted one. An overdose. An accident. Death by misadventure.

"You're probably right, those windows don't just crack."

I work through the day. Count the minutes as they pass, slowly, slowly. I look at my watch. Jack catches me and laughs.

"Don't tell me, your *muse* is waiting and you must cease the moment."

"That's *seize* the moment Jack. Not *cease*."

"Still you better see Amadeo before you leave tonight. If I were you, I'd try to look a bit more interested in your work. And that advice is absolutely free."

*****

Six hours of grinding, and a skipped lunch. I head up the stairs and into the front office. The room is decorated for comfort. The chairs are ample and soft. The colours are muted. The light is softened by an amber shade over an opaque bulb. Amadeo sits behind a large, tired desk. An automatic espresso machine sits on his filing cabinet. He motions for me to help myself.

"I'd love to, but I'm a bit pressed for time," I tell him.

Amadeo shrugs. He is actually Mr. Amadeo, as was his father before him. No one around here knows his first name. We all just call him Amadeo. He emigrated from Italy as a young teenager and yet still he seems out of place. His speech, his mannerisms, all point back to the Italian countryside. Urban Toronto has not made its mark on him and, after forty odd years of life here, it is doubtful that it ever will.

"You see," he begins, as though we were already in conversation, "you see, I love stone. I loved stones as a boy and collected them in my pockets. Sometimes my mother would do the laundry and scream at me because I forgot to take them out."

He laughs, shaking his large head from side to side. I look over to the espresso machine, regretting that I declined a cup. It's going to be a longer meeting than hoped.

"So of course I was the one to inherit the business, even though I was not the eldest."

"Did you have many brothers and sisters?" I ask him.

"Oh yes. Many! You?"

"An only child."

"Yes, I thought so."

And just when I think he is going to say those cliches about only children, how selfish we all are, how self-centered and egomaniacal we are, he surprises me. "Yes, you have that air of loneliness about you. It must be hard to be an only child. All the hopes and dreams of the parents falling on only one pair of shoulders. What do they think of your job choice?"

Instead of saying that my mother is dead and that my father stopped approving of me some time ago, I lie and tell him that they only want what is best for me.

"Do you think you have chosen what is best for you?"

"I'm an artist. There is no choice."

He nods. "When did you know that? Always?"

"No. It was when I first saw *The Barberini Faun*."

The Faun. I was thirteen when I first laid eyes on *The Barberini Faun*. He was lying back, supine, legs parted and on display. I was perhaps too young to understand the expression on his face, but it caught my imagination somehow and I understood without knowing.

My parents wanted to press on, there was so much to see at the *Glyptothek*, but I hung back. And, when their backs were turned, I crept over to him, not wanting to interrupt his rapture. I placed my hand on his hard marble leg. Felt along his muscles, lightly stroking him from calf to thigh.

A weakness I had never known seized me. I looked over my shoulder; the room was too busy with tourists and guards. I couldn't climb onto the rock. Couldn't nestle myself between those strong legs, or press my lanky body into that forbidden piece he so brazenly exposed. Oh God, how I needed to rest my head on the surface of his masculine stomach.

The mere thought produced a rush of excited dampness, an inner heat, and a pounding that could not be contained. Desire spoke to my body and my imagination. I was awakened by marble. There was no going back.

We stayed in Munich for three weeks. My father spent most of his time at the University and, at first, we waited in the hotel for his late afternoon return. I began to torment my mother in ways only a preteen can. Finally she broke down and asked, "What would you like to do today, Lexie?"

Thus began our daily visits with *The Barberini Faun*. My mother, hanging back and watching, as I studied and absorbed the marble god. She must have realized that the statue was changing me and that I was, slowly growing away from her.

I secretly masturbated throughout that entire trip. The first time I was filled with terror, and awe. I was exploring uncharted lands of my own body. I was able to affect my own sensations, my own responses. I was fascinated with the power I held over myself. Of course I feared that my parents suspected something every time they asked me how I slept.

When the family trip was over, I brought my passion home with me. September brought the beginning of high school. I made no friends. I watched as other girls giggled about high school boys, and wondered, why the fuss? They fantasized about kissing their mortal lips, weak lips while I dreamed of *The Barberini Faun,* remembering his perfection, his masculinity and his immortal surrender.

When my high school years finished I announced that I would study fine arts and become a sculptor. My father was horrified.

"How will you possibly make a living?" he asked.

But my mother sighed knowingly. She, at least, understood my ambitions without comprehending my desires. But she wouldn't live long enough to see me graduate. She would never witness my creations. She would never know if her sacrifices would ever amount to anything. And I would never give her the chance to be proud of me.

It is marble that awoke me. It is also marble that I fear most. I do not know which ancient Greek sculpted *The Barberini Faun,* but two thousand years after its creation it is, for me, a reminder of sexual awakening, death and exile. I do not tell Amadeo all of this. Only that I saw the sculpture in Munich and that it changed my life's path.

I wait for him to say something but Amadeo just sits looking at me. I fold my hands in my lap. Some stone dust has made its way under my collar but I do not scratch. Amadeo smiles at me. The irritation intensifies. That's it, I can no longer bear it. I pull at my shirt, ease the material from my throat.

"It's a mucky job," he finally says.

"Yes," I say. "It is a mucky job. Stone cutting isn't easy."

"No! Or we would all be Michelangelos!" he laughs. "Go on, you must have better things to do on a Friday night."

"Thank you," I say, raising myself from the cushioned seat. As I reach the door I turn back to him, sensing that somehow our exchange has been as unsatisfying to him as it has been bewildering to me.

"I do love stone," I tell him.

"I know. That's the only reason I keep you. Try to be on time tomorrow. We have five orders."

And with that I am free to go home, shower, and wait for my model.

*****

Premika arrives almost two hours late. I assume that there must have been a lot of silver subway trains that evening, but I don't ask.

"So. Should I just strip off now?" She's certainly direct.

"No. Not yet. There's plenty of time."

As eager as she seemed, I didn't want to rush it. Didn't want to merely create something in her likeness. It had to be more. I had to crack her shell, get inside her, and snatch up her soul. I had to penetrate her.

"Well?" she asks, "What will you use? Marble would be nice. Or you could cast me in bronze."

"Clay," I tell her, "clay."

Her soft pout almost breaks my heart. I want to tell her that I've lost my appetite for stone cutting; two years of engraving memorials has made me yearn for a more lively material. Something wet and pliable, tactile and messy. Something fertile, smelling of earth. Something more forgiving.

"You will be much more beautiful in clay. Softer, more feminine. Marble has been done. It's tired. If you want to be remembered, you have to use a different material. Something modern yet classic. Like you."

She smiles and begins unbuttoning her shirt. I put out my hand and catch hers in mine.

"No, not yet," I say firmly, "not yet."

*****

"Why not marble?" The question comes from Jack.

It's odd that Jack is not enthused about me working in clay when clay was the medium of his choice. He was obsessed with the construction of large, human-sized, earthen pots. Every few weeks he would go to his parent's farm, just north of Kleinburg, and he'd light an enormous bonfire in the middle of their field. Huge pots would be swallowed by the flames. Consumed, burned and solidified. Then he would start the glazing process. His finishes were extraordinary. The pots he showed me were whimsical, enormous and unlike anything I had ever seen. It was this process of his that I hoped he could do for my life size statue of Premika.

"It won't work. It can't be controlled. Every interesting glaze is in fact an accident. Half the pots don't even survive it. One tiny air bubble, or if the clay is too thick then the whole thing explodes. Naw, you should use wax and cast in bronze. Or better still, cut it in stone for something that big."

"I can't afford marble, let alone the equipment. And where would I sculpt it? In my loft? How would I get a huge marble up those stairs? Besides, I live there. The place would never be free of stone dust again!"

"You can cut it here. Use the equipment. Amadeo wouldn't mind. He'd love it in fact."

I ease myself onto a large granite slab. Stansford grey. Lovely veins without many speckles in the rock. I run my hand over the cool surface. It is an unintentional gesture. Jack chuckles.

"I don't get it. You love stone. Hell, I got you this job because you love it. And yet, you won't sculpt in marble. "

It's true. Without Jack I would still be unemployed, wondering how to pay my rent.

"*You* work in stone but you love clay. Why should it seem strange to you, of all people, that I would choose to use clay?" I ask him.

" 'Cause I don't call myself an artist. I really don't. A craftsman, maybe. I make pots in my spare time. It is what I do for fun. It amuses me."

"But when you create your pots, you use clay and so...."

"Look, I work in stone when I make a wall or a garden folly. Clay is the best material I know of for pots. Headstones should be made of granite or marble, not wax or clay. The right material for the right job. That simple."

"What are you trying to say?"

"A statue's gotta be marble or bronze. That's all."

"A sculpture can be anything. Bronze, clay, bubblegum with human hair, if you like!"

"Nope. Life size sculpture should be bronze or marble. You'll never stick it to that prick Boris if you use clay! He won't rate it! Besides, firing the damn thing will be problematic. First there is the hollowing it out aspect, did you think of that? Then you'll have to disassemble it just so it will fit in the kiln."

"But it can be done?" I persist.

Jack smiles. In six years of friendship he has learned that there is no point arguing with me once I have my heart set on something.

"It can be done. I s'pose. Still, I don't know why you'd want clay."

"Number one: There is no dust when you work in clay. No irritants under the bra. Your nostrils are filled with the smell of earth and not with dry, dry grit. Your hands shape and touch and coerce. Number two: Clay is feminine and cooperative. It is easier than marble, gentler than granite."

Jack laughs, not believing me.

"And three: Her skin is the colour of clay," I tell him.

I know that it is a near impossible feat. The balance must be perfect. The lines, just so. Fired clay is as vulnerable as it is strong.

"Besides, God thought clay was good enough to shape Adam..."

"Thought you didn't believe in God."

"I do when it's convenient."

Jack shrugs, "Clay it is then."

*****

I have spent many days with her, watching her, studying her every move, trying to capture that *something*. I have countless sketches now. I have finished two small maquettes. They are in her likeness but I am not satisfied. I cannot begin the main work until I have set the basic image in miniature.

"What time is it," she asks me.

"I don't know. Getting late."

"Well, that's just about it for me today."

She's restless now. I'll never get what I need from her. There's a world of difference between the woman stretched before me and the clay in my hands. I can't breathe life into it.

"Just a bit longer Premika," I beg.

"I really can't bear any more."

"Just stretch your leg a little longer in front of you. Point your toe to extend that line."

"No. I can't."

"Can't or won't?" I ask.

"Can't." She readjusts her position, breaks the pose. Tries to shake out her leg.

Of course she had become bored with the process. We had been working together for two weeks and I had nothing to show for it. She wanted instant immortality and her patience was wearing thin.

"I don't see why you can't just start the life size one. You keep mucking about with these little clay things. They look like dolls."

My hands press against the fragile shape of the miniature Premika, clay oozing between my fingers. Her image distorted. Another squeeze and it is completely destroyed.

"This piece of work cannot just *look* beautiful. It has to," I pause. "It must be so much more."

"God, you're starting to sound just like Boris. All concept. Next thing you know you will be looking for some political statement!"

I draw my clay-covered hand to my cheek. It's warm with a flushed reaction. Premika sees the blush and smiles. She gets up from her pose and reaches for her robe.

"So, tell me, when did it end for you?"

"What?"

"Your affair with Boris?"

I don't know why we're suddenly talking about Boris. I have noticed that when she is bored, or when I disappoint her, she turns the conversation to Boris. Somehow it amuses her even as it irritates me.

"Well he was your mentor after all."

"More like my tormentor."

Her robe is now fully on. She looks as lovely clothed as bare. The soft fabric drapes over her curves, suggesting the flesh beneath. Green silk. Green is her colour. But I don't work in colours, only shapes, and hers are highlighted by the cling of the folds of material.

"You do know he was fucking the two of us at the same time?" She picks up a half finished cup of coffee. Sips and makes a disappointed face.

"Hardly at the same time," I correct.

"Well, over the same period. We overlapped."

She walks into my kitchen, taking her mug with her. I have no choice but to follow her as she takes over my space, dumping her old coffee down the sink, reaching for the kettle, treating my kitchen as though it was her own.

"He adored you. Constantly told me how brilliant he thought you were."

"Boris? You've got to be joking!" I dismiss her. The idea was ridiculous. "You know, he never mentioned you. I used to ask him about you but, nothing." I mean to hurt her by that remark but it barely touches her. The barb grazes her gently and she shrugs it off. My mosquito bite, my tiny scratch. Boris is, to Premika, a link between us. Something shared.

"Of course he didn't mention me. But I knew about you the whole time. I once found your panties beside his bed," she laughs. Then there is no more talk as she concentrates on grinding some coffee. Just the whirr of the blades against the beans.

"Don't you think that's odd?" I ask.

"Not at all! Men can only manage one true love at a time, the rest are, you know, friends. Friends with benefits." She continues, pouring boiling water now into my chipped bodum.

"Which was I?"

"Which do you think, silly?"

I shrug my shoulders. Does it matter now? I would like to believe that I'd moved on but, if I had, why was it so important to impress him with my work? Perhaps we always seek approval from the father, the mentor and the critic. Why? Why do we let men define us?

"Look, a man can confide in his mistress because he has no fear of losing her. His true love he protects with a shield of guile." She smiles at her own cleverness but I know that the quote belongs to Boris.

"So when did *you* stop seeing him?"

Premika waves her hand in the air dismissively. Her gesture implies it had been some time ago but her silence implies something other. Her response is filled with guile and I can't help but wonder whom she is protecting.

CHAPTER 4

Every time there is a delay, people speculate. Some say there's a jump almost every week. Some say there are more. Some say that Monday mornings are the worst. I suppose that staring ahead at a full work week could be overwhelming. But others think it is Wednesday. The get-over-the-hump day.

A voice sounds over the loudspeaker, reciting a code, a series of numbers. It could be a malfunction or a power failure. It doesn't have to be a suicide. It's not always a suicide. A train could be out of service. That's all.

"Oh God," a man says, looking at his watch.

I stand well behind the yellow line. I wait. The impatient man with the watch decides to leave. Hail a taxi, perhaps, instead. The dynamics change when he goes. He may be gone but he has left his impatience behind him. It spreads across the platform. Strangers start to talk to one another. To tell each other where they should be and how very awful it is that they'll be late. Knowing looks and knowing sighs. They bond with their impatience.

I am on my way to Premika's. I am not panicked. She is never ready when I arrive and, no matter how late I might be, she always greets me with, "Oh, you're here already?" Tonight we are going to a new club. It just opened. Premika knows the owners; she's on the list. She says it is very important to be on the list from the start. Once a club is known there's no point. The height of its popularity is the beginning of it becoming passé. Who wants to be seen in a place that isn't on the climb?

I check my watch. If I spend money on a taxi then I won't have any left for drinks. I'll wait here with the others. Premika's always, always late.

*****

The dance floor is packed with an early crowd. We squeeze past the bodies, making our way to the centre, all the while breathing the scent of dancers' sweat and second hand smoke. The room is a haze with bodies moving in the fractured light.

How did we get in so quickly? Skip the line-up, not queuing. Pass the hopefuls. Walk to the front, and approach a very substantial bouncer. Premika knows him. He kisses her on both cheeks, waves us in. It's much the same with the bartender. A light kiss on each cheek, two tequila shooters. And then two more.

As the second shooter flies down my throat, I feel the room move. Then I am possessed. This other woman creeps in, takes over my body. Not words, an act. Time to dance.

Premika catches my eye. We leave the bartender, promising to see him again. Promises, promises. But no commitments. She takes my hand, leads me to the dance floor, to face the music.

We are very different dancers. Premika is sensual and almost graceful. Her moves are premeditated, choreographed. She lifts her arms over her head and moves her hips like a Spanish Toreador. Then she struts and runs her fingers through her hair. She varies her moves but the pout never leaves her lips.

Premika doesn't sweat when she dances. I am the opposite. Sweat pours off my body. My hair dampens and curls around my temples and nape of my neck, as I throw myself around the dance floor, twisting and turning. That other woman has total possession of me now. She goads me to dance harder. I oblige until I am breathing hard and gasping for air. I slow my rhythm to catch my breath, but my feet don't stop moving, my shoulders keep shimmying and in no time I'm whipped back into a frenzy. Completely out of touch with reality. A million miles away from my work, my ideals, myself.

The D.J. starts a medley of old rock'n roll tunes. That's Premika's cue. She grabs me and cuts through the other dancers, heads for the stage. She jumps up and gestures for me to follow. The crowd cheers. We dance together, for each other and for the others looking at us, watching. A young man leaps up and moves between us. He's agile and flexible. Everything about him is intense, dark. Dark eyes, dark hair, swarthy complexion. He dances in an athletic, masculine manner, somehow bridging the gap between Premika and me. His dance blends us, then separates us. Now dancing with one and then the other. Giving us equal time with no sense of favouritism.

Three figures dancing together, each looking at the other.

*****

I remember that night in a blur of pentimento detail. At times I wasn't sure which of us he was kissing. We seemed somehow integrated, one person. Then his hand would move over the contours of my face, his fingers finding my mouth, separating my teeth. And I knew at that moment he was kissing her.

It was an ornate mosaic, the most vibrant and intense moments filling me, etching into my memory. All else receding into the background of sensation. I remember biting into a knuckle. Then his lips moved away from hers and pressed into mine. His fingers still at play, entering and re-entering my mouth. His other hand mapping a tour of her soft curves; I heard a plaintive breath escape her. Felt her body shift in the bed. The sheets slipped away. Then he was inside me. I turned to watch Premika as he penetrated me. Her eyes were half closed and an angel's smile played on her mouth. His hand had found its way up between her long thighs. She anticipated his touch.

I moved my hips upwards to meet him, slipped a pillow under my bum. Took more of him in. I ran my nails over his back. I never took my gaze from her whether he was concentrated on me or Premika. It was as if he were the glue between us.

*****

Premika and I are tucked into bed together. My bed. Why she insisted that we should come to my place instead of hers, I do not know. All I know is that she has remained in my bed.

Our dancer had been reluctant to leave but eventually Premika convinced him to go.

"Staying the night," she said to him, "would be far too intimate."

"But I have just made love to you both. What could be more intimate than that?"

"Sleeping!" She replied, pushing him, barely dressed, out the door.

There is a radiance about Premika. A glow. The sex has been washed from her body. The night's adventures have spiraled down the drain. She has slipped into one of my oversized, white, cotton

t-shirts. She looks innocent, fresh. Untouched.

My shower hasn't quite sobered me. The water hasn't broken through the bacchanal haze. I exist somehow between her world and mine and can make sense of neither. What happened tonight, and how can she lie there so casually, so unaffected?

She puts her cold feet on my side of the bed. Warms them against me. The crazy drinking and the sharing of a man hasn't fooled me though. I know there is a gold statue inside her.

There is something more than the desire for sensation and the quest for fun. She is so much more than she appears. She must be. She has to be. I want to tell her this but the penumbra overtakes me and I feel myself drifting from her. My body, light now, lifting from the bed and floating out of touch. I give myself over to sleep, believing that all things are possible and, as I slip away, I find myself nearing that point on the horizon. The place where all things meet. Infinity.

*****

Infinity. Without a beginning or an end. A work that has no front, no back and no determined sides. Every part equal. Every inch, every millimeter, valid, intrinsic, worthy.

Get up!

But it's dark outside, and the bed is so comfortable. Beside me Premika sleeps; her body's warm and fragrant. I snuggle down, firmly close my eyes.

Get up!

Three bodies, somehow connected, each leading to the next. His cock inside me, my hand holding hers, her lips meeting his. The key to the spiraling vortex. The image won't leave me. I get up.

Premika sleeps on, unaware that a voice inside my head screams for me to abandon her. Her arm lies heavily across my stomach like a dead weight. I lift it gently, so as not to disturb her, and place it softly beneath the sheets. I rise from the bed and fumble around for my robe. A few hangers clatter to the ground. Premika doesn't stir. She remains as I left her, her hair spread out over my pillow, loose and unadorned. Such hair need not be fashioned.

I close the bedroom door and creep into my cramped workspace. I search through the many reference and art books piled one on top of the other on my shaky, overburdened bookshelf. I thumb through pages, dog-eared and marked with clay fingerprints. How can I create a piece with no beginning and no end. A piece as infinite as love.

Finally I find the image I'm searching for. *The Rape of the Sabine Woman*. Nothing rivals *The Rape of the Sabine Woman*. It is a work of tension and drama. From one angle it is savage and cruel, another seems almost forgiving and merciful, but then the sculpture turns violent again. It is a perfectly balanced asymmetrical masterpiece. Three contrasting figures twist and turn, united in one common action. Rape. What inspired Giovanni Bologna to create something of this magnitude? Why did he smash his hammer against his chisel until an abducted woman and two lust driven men emerged from the marble? The act of rape becomes art, a thing of beauty. That is the alchemy of it. The unfathomable change from what is base to what is precious. From metal to gold. From pain to art. And rape is lifted beyond its base act and transformed. Immortalized.

Three figures. No beginning and no end. *A spiraling vortex.* I roll my sleeves up, prepare to start. My monument will be clay, not marble. Clay, only because it is what I have on hand, this moment. My piece will not be mammoth and overbearing like *The Rape of the Sabine Woman*, but rather delicate and inviting. Three figures together, connected through the act of lovemaking. Each figure looking at the other, moving around a spiraling vortex. Every turn of the sculpture will hold a different meaning, just as the night held a different expectation for each of us. Every angle of the sculpture will be a different image to the eye. The piece will not only be an homage to our lovemaking but also an homage to that earlier artist. *Giovanni, this one's for you.*

I somehow knew, even before we were fucking, when we were dancing perhaps, that I would freeze the moment in time. I was aware of the magic of three figures. Sculpture is always more interesting in odd numbers. A single body, a lover's triangle.

I grab up my tools and throw myself into my work. Nothing else exists but the clay. My breath fills with its earthy aroma. My touch awakens with its leathery texture. A curve of the neck, a hollow of the back. Three Figures, each looking at the other, around and around a spiraling vortex.

I press on the clay and it gives way to my fingers. It submits to my touch. Yields to my will. The figures begin to take corporeal form. They are enraptured, yielding and desirous. They are all three surrendering to the moment. Giving themselves over. And yet, from another angle they appear avaricious and self serving. And then, with another turn, they are benign once again. Loving and carefree. Three Figures. Each independent, but existing only in context of the other two.

Here they are, almost breathing and in full motion. Not yet detailed but certainly there, in shape, in feel, in attitude. Myself, a bit hesitant perhaps and looking at her. The young man, a beautiful shape still lacking in features. His body belongs to her. And then Premika, touched by the man, watched by me, is the glue. Even as she looks away.

I suddenly remember the woman asleep in my bed. What time is it now? Morning? Perhaps I should wake her with a coffee? Serve her in bed?

I cover over the damp clay, wipe my hands and head over to the galley kitchen. But Premika is already awake and up, perched on a stool, sipping a coffee she has made herself. I pick up the kettle. Still warm, so I fix myself an instant coffee and join her. She waves a scrap of paper at me at laughs.

"What's that?" I ask her.

"Max."

"Max? Was that his name?"

"Yes. Do you think he's a Maxwell?"

"Maximilian?" I suggest.

"He left his number. I wonder which of us he intended it for..."

I shrug and reach for the paper. She snatches it up. Holds it from my grasp.

"Silly boy," she begins to rip it slowly. "Doesn't he realize it was just for fun?"

"Maybe he wanted to have fun again?" I venture.

"Once is fun. Twice is repetition. And three times is a relationship." She tosses the scraps over her shoulder. "I would have made you a cup, but I didn't want to interrupt you when you were working. How is it?"

She looks happy and lovely and in my kitchen. She thinks I've been working on her piece. Getting on with it.

"Coming along," I yawn.

"You should get some sleep," she suggests. "I'll come by later if you want."

Before she asks to see what I've done, I usher her to the door. I lean against its frame and watch as she makes her way down the steep stairs. I won't tell Premika about the three figures. She would see it as a betrayal. Me working on another vision when I should be concentrating solely on her. I have no choice but to pretend that I am happy with my miniatures and ready to move onto the life sized piece. I'll still have to wait for the huge order of clay to be delivered. There is still a large armature to build to hold the piece. I must let on that we are close with the maquettes. This will keep her happy. Keep her coming.

Only when she exits the front door, only when she is out of sight, do I close my own apartment door. All alone now, I kneel to pick up the pieces of our discarded lover.

*****

Sun streams through the floor to ceiling windows of Premika's twelfth story. A bead of sweat clings darkly on her brow before making its way over her high cheekbone. It rolls across her honeyed skin, languidly mapping the contours of her face. She changes postures and stretches catlike into the Bow. I'm still doing the Sun Salutation. It's warm. And Premika is so lovely.

Yoga is Premika's newest craze. She extols its virtues as though it were the true religion. She sees it as a mind, spirit, and body connection. One that will stop, or at least stall, the signs of aging. And so we stretch our bodies; I've never stretched more than my imagination before. I concentrate, but my movement is shaky, my poses awkward. Premika, however, moves through a series of postures as though performing a well practiced dance. How can she be so good at this already? She's just taken it up!

I stretch some more, pretending to know what I'm doing. Premika reaches her arms in front of her, aligns her head and sends her bum high into the air, completing her pose. I point and flex my bare feet. Shake out my legs.

"What's that pose then?"

"Downward dog," she exhales. "I'm going to Paris for a while. I meant to tell you before. I've been offered a new contract and I thought I'd stay for the spring collections. Do some ramp work."

"But I thought you already had an exclusive contract."

Premika releases her pose. Reaches her arms up to the sky. Why can't she pose so confidently for me?

"It hasn't been renewed. Besides, could be a game changer."

"Change isn't all it's cracked up to be."

Premika relaxes and laughs. "That from someone who changes her name as often as I change my clothes! Alex to me. Alexandra to Boris. Lexie to your mother."

"My mother is dead," I remind her. I'm not sure why I say this. I use my words as though they're weapons, as though the fact that my mother is dead should hurt her. But it is I who feels the pain. Doubly. One blow because Premika is leaving, another because my mother is dead.

"At least you knew both your parents. My father abandoned me."

She exhales on the window glass. Traces her fingers in the mist. Draws a heart.

"I'm sorry," I start but she waves me off.

"It was before I was born," she shrugs, now trying to sound casual about it. "He asked my mother to join him in India. She tried, but she couldn't take the crowds. She felt claustrophobic. I'm sure her pregnancy nausea didn't help any. They argued about it. He didn't want to live in Quebec, she didn't want to live there so the great love affair ended. The only reminder of it is me. A burp after a good curry," she laughs ironically. "You know what Premika means?"

"No."

"Lover... But it was also the name of a famous racehorse. He bet on that racehorse, but he wouldn't take a chance on my mom. Just a bump and tickle, but here I am."

I look away from her, stare down to the pavement below. So far to the ground. I place my hand on the warmth of the window. The glass is sturdy. Double glazed. A window like this wouldn't give way, it would have to be opened or smashed first.

"Do you have to go?" I ask, facing the real issue upsetting me.

She shrugs me off. "I won't be gone for long. A month, six weeks at the most. And we can work until I go. I'm not leaving right away. We have some time."

"Yes," I say, suddenly aware that there can be no more procrastination. The process must now take its course. "Let's make a schedule. Be disciplined."

*****

A hush has fallen over my studio. My tools are laid out like a surgeon's: cleaned, organized, and ready. I have three completely finished maquettes in varying sizes. The last one, the final one before I sculpt her life-size doppelgänger, stands just over a foot in height. She is quite detailed for a maquette. Her face and hands more defined than most blueprints. I could fire this one, cover her with an unusual glaze and be done with it. Forget about the work I had intended. Just move on to the next idea. I have spent too long on this puzzle, at the cost of all other work. But this maquette, this small offering, isn't the opus I need to answer Boris's challenge.

Why should it matter? My father's opinion no longer matters. Distance is the great band-aid on the wound of disregard. Unlike Boris, he has no opinion of art and so I cannot expect him to comment on my work. But Boris, who entered my life just after my father exited it, has opinions. Before he had his own gallery he wrote art reviews for three different magazines. He advised gallery owners, worked as a curator and was flown yearly to Brazil where he attended an international curator's conference. Boris's opinion matters because he is my only connection to the larger art world. And yet, Boris is my enemy. He is every curator, every arts council juror and every critic who takes a fashionable stance against beauty. A stance that seems to be spreading like a tumor across the face of Western aesthetics.

I remember some pillow talk I once had with Boris. We had just made love and, as was our wont, began our usual argument about my creative pursuits. He said I was wasting my time and talent because my work didn't reflect the burden of present day life. In response I called him a fascist. He was furious.

"My parents were refugees from Hitler's Europe! You can't say that! You just can't!"

"Your use of art is fascistic! Fascism bends art to its own purpose. It becomes a representation of an ideal. You want art to have a mandate, a purpose beyond its intrinsic value. Stalin had social realism, Hitler had his *volk kunst*, and you have your mishmash of Bauhaus, phony left wing politics and I don't know what!"

Boris was speechless. He jumped up, grabbed my clothes and threw them out the window.

"Out! Out!" he ordered.

"You're joking."

"Now!"

It is surprising that he wanted to see me again after that. Even after we ended things he still wanted my opinions as much as I wanted his approval. But now I've thrown down the glove. Said I would prove him wrong, believing I could with the help of Premika's beauty. But Premika is going away.

*****

"Do you think that you might cast it in bronze when it's done?"

"No." My voice is firm but I am really starting to question my choice. What if clay is not the right medium? Gods, heroes and icons have been immortalized in marble. Great warriors and leaders have been replicated in bronze. And no-one, it seems, supports me in my choice of clay.

Premika seems out of place in my space. Perhaps because it is a true loft space with a large radiant heater attached to the ceiling in the corner, work materials everywhere, and a bicycle I rarely use hanging on the wall. For Premika, this is not the way a grown up should live.

"So you're really going to leave it in clay, are you? I thought we agreed that you would think about casting it in bronze," Premika presses me.

"No we didn't. What do you mean? I never said that?"

"Well, don't you just use the clay to shape it and then you send it to a foundry or something? I mean, you aren't planning on showing it in clay, are you?"

She goes over to my work table and picks up a minute piece of clay. Holds it between her fingers then presses the tips together. She regards the smudge on her fingers with disdain and looks for something she can wipe them on.

"Do you know how rare it is to exhibit a life size terracotta? How hard it is to balance, to defy gravity?"

"Of course it's rare. Who wants to be turned into a great big old pot?" Premika leans up against the wall then slowly slides down on to her haunches, a look of utter disbelief and disgust on her face.

"It will be a finished, delicate work in terra-cotta. You know the Greeks worked in clay as often as marble, but we only consider the marble because the gods were always..."

"Oh fuck off with your Greek lectures! You're turning me into a piece of pottery! Should have just put me on one of those wheelie things you potters use. It would have been a lot quicker!"

"You haven't a clue," I say, "do you know what bronze costs? Do you know how much it would be to cast a life sized figure? You think I have that kind of money?"

"Are you angry?" she asks.

"Yes!"

"At me?"

"Yes."

"Because you can't afford to cast in bronze? That's my fault?"

"No," I say slowly and with deliberation, "I'm angry because you called me a potter!"

"Well, you *are* making me out of... muck. Just name one great statue that was made in clay," she challenges.

"Silenus. He was made of clay."

There was reason for this, and it wasn't because the Greeks hated the discomfort of stone dust. It wasn't because they were too insecure to pick up the chisel. *Silenus* was made of clay because clay could be left hollowed. In that hollow was placed a perfect little golden sculpture of the demigod. The clay represented all that was earthy and sensual about him while the gold hidden inside was his daemon. His true godly essence. Not the wild drunk horseman who is so easy to recognize, but that part of *Silenus* that is a divine being. A being that is revealed only through the touch of Eros or the breaking of clay.

"Never heard of him. Can't be that famous."

"Trust me," I tell her, "you just have to trust me on this one."

How can I ask that of her when my maquettes are lacking, lifeless. I know it's because they don't contain Premika's daemon. I have not captured her soul yet. It is beyond my grasp, somewhere on the borders of infinity.

*****

Infinitely more people jump from the Golden Gate Bridge in San Francisco than from the Oakland Bay Bridge. Why? Why choose one bridge over the other? Is it because of the view? The Bay Bridge joins two very urban, concrete settings while the Golden Gate stretches between two prettier, more panoramic views. Suspended over the Pacific, one side of the bridge offers the lights of San Francisco, small and benign in the distance, while the other side overlooks Alcatraz, a lonely rock bashed by tireless waves. Perhaps in choosing the Golden Gate the suicide chooses a more poetic ending. The civilized world has failed him and in those last few seconds, as he steps off the edge, he takes in a moment of beauty and carries it away with him over the River Styx.

Both bridges are known to natives and travelers. They are the Gateway to what is arguably America's most beautiful city. But the Golden Gate is mythic. It is a common setting in movies, mysteries and love stories. People from all over the world go to see the Golden Gate Bridge because it has something lyrical, dreamy and romantic about it. It has the legacy of those who have gone before. The Bay Bridge has no legacy. It is like a silver subway train. There is no sense of history to it. No sense of a past.

I only have fragments of Premika's past. There are secrets she keeps from me. I can only imagine her history, the places she's been, the lovers she's had. Is the imagination greater than the reality? Is my interpretation of her closer to her soul than the image she projects of herself? How to make a work that will be as mythic as the Golden Gate Bridge? As iconoclastic, eternal and beckoning? How to make a solid representation of a siren's song?

*****

"Are you in love with her?"

Boris is leaning back in his chair, relaxed. His jacket is off. He's drinking his afternoon tea. There are two biscuits on his saucer. He offers me one.

"What makes you ask that?" I try to sound casual as I bite into the bland digestive biscuit.

"You're preoccupied. You know, I think you're guilty of breaking the cardinal rule."

"And what is that?"

"You've fallen in love with your model," Boris laughs. "So? Have you broken her open? Found her soul? Discovered her darkest secrets?"

How is it that Boris always seems to know where I am in my creative process? How is it that he can see my every obstacle, my every creative block? Sometimes he really pisses me off!

"You're the one who broke the cardinal rule with her, not me."

"You are quite wrong. I never loved her. And the fucking was entirely her idea, not mine."

I want to focus on something else, change the topic. I would ask him about the gallery, but there are bare walls all around Boris. He's between shows. Unlike other gallery owners, Boris will not fill his gallery unless he feels it is a show worthy of his space. And so, in his soft gray cashmere sweater and charcoal trousers, he is the only thing on display here.

"How do you make a living ? You should have your artists booked one after the other?"

"Don't be bourgeois, it doesn't become you."

"Are you still teaching?"

"Not so much now, but that's my choice. The academic world was getting too comfortable. I was becoming an academic, like the rest of those twits. Dusty, dry, out of touch. Not good. You start living only through your student's work. So I am strictly part time now." He smiles fondly at me. "So? Haven't you gotten bored with her yet?"

"What makes you ask that?"

"She's narcissistic and you have a short attention span. A.D.D. or whatever the newest label is. Everything is a disorder these days. I suppose Premika has D.D.D.," he laughs.

"What's that?"

"Depth-deficit-disorder."

"It's funny," I snap at him, "that you never spoke of her before. You pretended that you couldn't remember her. Now you can't shut up about her!"

"Tell me something," he speaks slowly and quietly. Even his body leans closer and the chair swivels forward to accommodate him, "has she mentioned her father at all?"

"I know all about her father."

Boris lifts an eyebrow. Studies me. And then very slowly, very deliberately he says, "Yes. And do you know that she told him that if he didn't come here to meet her that she would kill herself? And he said," Boris wobbles his head and attempts an East Indian accent, "'Go kill yourself then.' He knew it was just a threat. I suppose it's the only time she didn't get whatever man she wanted. Or woman, as the case may be."

Boris gets up, walks around his desk, then plants a kiss on my forehead. There is no sexuality in it.

"Just be careful," he says. Then he walks to the door and opens it for me.

*****

The large, temporary armature is now constructed, ready to support the more delicate limbs and to provide balance. The wooden table is cleared. Here we begin. First I must wedge close to 500 lbs. of clay. Smash it against the wood of the table. Throw it down. Banish every possible hidden air pocket, then knead it into submission. Some of the clay will remain firmer. This clay I will use to build up and then carve away, almost like stone.

Only two weeks of work before Premika leaves for Paris. We meet every other day in my tiny, cramped studio. Premika is perfectly beautiful in her nakedness, but I am uninspired.

Inspiration: to breathe in. Do I create as much from my lungs as I do from my heart or my brain? If I breathe deeper, inhale her distinct aroma, will the spark of inspiration ignite the flames of my creativity?

"You love me, don't you?"

Premika is stretching before me. A Daphne, arms to the heavens, escaping the rape of Apollo. I want her to reach more, to tense to the point of snapping. To the point where nymphs transform into immortal shapes. A tree, a reed, a river.

Every sculptor has his definitive piece. One might argue that Bernini's *David* or his *St. Theresa* defined his work, but I would disagree. Bernini is summed up in his depiction of *Apollo and Daphne.* Her hands metamorphosing into leaves as she reaches, reaches away from Apollo's desire.

I spritz the clay. It glistens with the new moisture. My hands move easily over the surface now. There is almost a rhythm to the work. A dance between me and the red earth.

She stretches her arms above her head. Her torso lengthens, her skin becomes more taut. An outline of ribs appear beneath a layer of flesh. How should she be remembered? A woman stretches before me, but for what is she reaching? To be remembered, laurels are needed. A crown of immortality, the leaves of a victor, the whispering words, *remember thou art mortal*. She reaches. I could place the laurels of my affection at her feet but would she notice them? Or would she just reach, reach away. It is so close. So close to what I need.

She discards her pose. Relaxes. Sits back on her haunches and laughs. She laughs and the moment is gone, the pose is lost.

Of course I *was* in love with her. She was beauty incarnate. Unmarred. Unflawed. A goddess. She wore her hair loose and her perfume liberally. Even when she posed naked she wore it, lightly and airily. Deliberately on her throat along the jugular vein, behind her ears or knees or ankles. Sprayed across those translucent wrists, at the base of her bony spine. Or dabbed at the top of her groin.

Of course I was in love with her. But she was in love with herself. Not a Daphne, then, at all. But Narcissus. An unsupported flower, tottering on its thin stem.

"That's why you are taking so long to sculpt me."

She makes for her robe but before she reaches it I snatch it up. She stands naked before me. Her face has the look of an exasperated parent. She puts her hand out, expecting me to obey, to hand it over because she commands it.

"Did you want this?" I ask her.

She says nothing, just waits with an outstretched arm.

"None of the miniatures feel right. I haven't found *it* yet."

"It? All of the miniatures look great. I would be happy with any of them. They're all really good!"

"Your eye is too easily fooled. You're used to slumming it with Boris and other two dimensional painters. Sculpture is three-dimensional. It is tactile. Come here."

She drops her hand. Takes a step forward. I take her hand in mine and lead her touch to the damp, leathery figure of a small maquette. I guide her fingers over the small breasts of the statuette, I press the palm of her hand into its slightly rounded stomach, and I push the flesh of her thumb into its innocent ribs. Premika keeps her gaze leveled on me. She's too curious to object, so I take her hand from the cold clay statuette and bring it to the warmth of her body.

"The hand longs to go where the eyes have already been," I trace the same route along *her* surface now. Her hands mapping her breasts, her belly, her ribs. "It is a tactile medium. The clay has to be alive. It must be flesh of your flesh. It can't just look like you; it has to feel like you. It has to *be* you."

Premika takes her robe from me. I wait for her to dress, but instead she unfastens the sash and steps toward me.

"Turn around," she orders.

I obey and she ties the silk around my eyes in a blindfold. She takes my hand and leads me away. Across the studio floor, through the kitchen and into my room.

"You've spent too long looking at me," she says.

She pulls me down so I'm sitting beside her on my bed. I know her body is sprawled over my sheets, her hair is spilling on my pillows but I am denied the image.

"Go ahead, explore." Then she quotes me back to myself, "It can't just look like me, it has to *feel* like me."

I reach past the sheets until my hand touches flesh. Soft, warm, taut. I spread my fingers, wrap them around a hipbone. Then they work over her stomach, discover her navel, and pause. I am unable to move, to choose a direction. I hover over her stomach, barely touching now, skimming her surface. My hand hardly strokes her. I am immobilized. Then her hand guides mine down until I feel the downy rise of her pubic bone.

"It's okay," she whispers, "the hand longs to go where the eyes have already been. Go ahead."

I slide the tips of my fingers along her, trace the edges of her wet opening. Yes, this is where to begin. This is the gateway to her secrets. This is the key to what has been hidden from me. My fingers press inside. Premika's breath is audible, quickened. She tenses and presses herself toward my hand. I slow my movements, wait for her cue. She quietly moans with impatience. Her hands brush mine and I know she is opening herself to me, pulling away her skin, making herself more accessible. I resume, intensifying my motion. Quickening. Pressing harder. Touching her as I would myself. And as her body quakes in a spasm of pleasure, my clay-worked fingers move inside her to feel the contractions of her inner being.

Premika sighs, hushes to a quiet rest. And yet, even in this state of submission and repose she has power over me. This is it! How could I have missed it? It was right in front of me, playing with me, but because I was afraid of it, because it made me feel inept and awkward, I had ignored it. Yes. It is the power of submission mixed with ecstasy that will make this sculpture great. Premika must appear to be awakening from her sleep, spent and ethereal but still ravenous to experience life. Wanting more even though she is already sated. Her image will enjoy the pleasure of herself without guilt. Bask in herself. Bask in the beauty of her goddess-like projection. Divine female spirit. And I will call her the Imago Dei. No. *The Imaga Dea.*

I lift my fingers to my nose and breathe in the scent of inspiration.

CHAPTER 5

Eight silver subway trains have passed and I wait patiently for a red. A foolish ritual I've adopted since she went away. Away to Paris. Paris in March. Paris in spring. But winter in Toronto.

If I let this silver train pass by, will it bring her back?

She had to go. Already I see advertisements with her face replaced. A pale, androgynous woman with cat's eyes and Bowie hair spraying her belly with Premika's perfume. How does it feel to be replaced?

Another silver train passes me by. Perhaps they know that she left and in their ennui decided not to run any more red trains. No. No. No. I must be patient. There will be another red train. She will come back.

The day she left for Paris she called me. Didn't want me to see her off. Said she must push me from her mind, get on with things. I agreed and said, "Of course, I understand."

I tried to get on with my work. I counted the days. But then I'd go to the corner grocery and I'd flip through a magazine. I'd pass by a billboard. Someone would have a television on. And she would be there, smiling. Smiling for everyone. Everywhere for everyone but nowhere for me. Of course she could push me from her mind. For her it was easy. I wasn't ubiquitously present.

Sometimes I would rest my hand on a glossy flat surface, a surface that was her. But there were no curves, no goose flesh in the cold. And if I just traced the line of her back, the memory in my finger tips would recall her. Recall the time when I couldn't shape the clay quite right and she took my hand in hers to guide me over her skin. How it reacted to the coolness of my touch. How her nipples shrank back and hardened from the unexpected cold. Was it? Then I left an incriminating trail of clay across her clavicle. I left my fingerprints on her body, but she pushed me from her mind.

I missed her because we were spending so much time together. I missed her because I needed her to pose for the sculpture. I missed her.

How many silver trains can there possibly be?

My toes stay well behind the line. There is at least two feet between me and the gash in which the tracks are laid. The mice still move between the tracks without fear, scurrying about their business. And on the platform the people are scurrying too. There is much business to be done. Time must be filled because if there is an opening, a space or a crack then one might pause to think. And there is one thought. One thought from which we run, from which we barricade ourselves. We fill our hours with activities, acquisitions and desires. We make things important. We give weight and meaning to all sorts of things. Anything but that one thought. The thought that our existence is pointless.

At last a very old red TTC train. I pick up my chisels, my satchel and myself and take a seat facing backwards.

*****

My late arrival is met with a glare of disapproval.

"Sorry Jack," I say. But Jack goes back to his stencils.

"There was a delay on the subway," I start to explain, but stop myself. Why lie to Jack? I walk over to his workstation and crouch down beside him.

"I am sorry. I know I let you down. I'm not myself."

"No, you aren't. You're sloppy and depressed. I don't know what's wrong with you. I'm starting to get worried about you."

"Thanks," I squeeze his thigh.

"Get over it," he finally says. "It doesn't matter how you do it. Go out, get laid, start another piece of work. Do anything, 'cause right now, you're no good to anyone."

Jack's right. I am numb. Existing without passion while I just count the days and wait for her return. It's been almost two months and I've heard nothing from her. I need to breathe in her absence, to work on something more inspiring than Amadeo's headstones and plaques. But how? How to work without a muse?

Jack touches my elbow, "Got a surprise for you. Might cheer you up. It's in the front room."

He leads me out of the workspace and into the public area. Here the stones are displayed. Clients will, in their grief, walk between these wordless, blank tablets, attempting to make the right choice. I remember a visit from one of Amadeo's sons. The two men talked and talked, not noticing that the small grand-daughter had climbed up on a tall stone. She started dancing, mocking death as only children can, like the Mexican children on the day of the dead. A woman, a client, was choosing a stone for her newly departed husband, and, seeing the child's dance, began to laugh. She couldn't stop herself. She became hysterical. With embarrassment she apologized and Amadeo's son tried to lift the girl from the stone. The little girl fought free, pointed at the woman and sang, "I'm the king of the castle and you're the dirty rascal." Amadeo's son grabbed his daughter and began to scold her, slapping her bottom. "No leave her," the woman said, "she is an angel from God."

"Over there." Jack points to something behind the new row of granite headstones. Something rough, unpolished. Freshly harvested. It's raw, irregular and waiting for someone to take it, cut into it and release the angel inside. Marble.

"Good God, Jack."

"Beautiful, eh?"

"I can't believe you bought that."

"I didn't. Amadeo did. He just doesn't know it yet."

I touch the stone, sweep my fingers across its unfinished exterior. There is a gentle vein colouring the stone. Bluish. It runs the length of the stone. It is deep beneath the surface. What could be done with the vein? How to use it?

"No-one's going to come in here and ask for this stone. Not unless it's cut and polished," I say. "Besides, most people would think that the vein is a flaw."

"I know. Looks like you got yourself a marble."

I stare in disbelief. How much could that have cost? Why would he buy it, or rather have Amadeo buy it, for me?

"What will you do with it?" Jack asks.

"Well, we have to see what plans Amadeo has. He did pay for it. Besides, I have some other work to finish first."

Jack pushes himself up on a stone, balances as though on a perch. "Don't take too long. I'd say that this was harvested about a month ago so you only have a matter of a few months. Eight at most."

He's right. Marble is quite yielding when it's first harvested. Not as difficult to cut as one imagines. Fresh out of a quarry, you can cut it by hand. It hardens with time, makes the sculptor's job more difficult. Eventually almost impossible. This stone is newly born, untouched. Judging by its surface density I figure it would be at least six to ten months until it would harden to the point where electric grinders and machines would be required instead of a sculptor's hammer and chisel.

"I can't do anything else on *The Imaga Dea*. Not until Premika comes back. I do have another piece that's close. I need a male model though."

"You're not asking me, are you?"

"No Jack, I wouldn't want to start objectifying you."

"No, 'cause then you'd have to sleep with me, and then it would get mucky 'cause you like me too much. And your art would suffer 'cause you like falling in love with your models, which is really strange because we both see how it destroys you..."

"Seduce and destroy share the same root in Greek. Did you know that?"

"Funny, but I didn't know that. There must be a big hole in my education," he jokes.

I picture the *Three Figures* in my head. Imagine Premika's body, vibrant and lithe, commanding the other two bodies, enjoying both equally. And the other female body, my own, focussed on her, reaching for her and yet accommodating the unfinished man. Why can't I conjure him fully, finish the work?

"I'll get to it this weekend. Finish it up."

"Great," says Jack. "If you need it fired, let me know. I'd like to fire up one more time before it gets too warm."

Jack hops off the stone. He's wiry and limber. Perhaps he could be the third figure after all. Stand in for the original. No, no, Jack's right. It would get too mucky.

I reach for my protective eye goggles. Back to the grindstone. Grinding stone.

*****

It was just a piece of rock! A hard and unyielding substance. It will not move and submit to my most gentle coaxing. Only an act of aggression could force a shape, a face or a figure into that marble. That marble. That exquisite marble.

Michelangelo would not force his vision upon his stone. No, he believed that the figure was trapped inside the rock and his job was to chisel and carve until he could release the angel within the rock. More stunning even than the *David* is a series of figures struggling to cast off the weighty marble surrounding their bodies. Each seems a Sisyphus, eternally fated to struggle against the great rock that traps the soul. As you walk between the two rows of statues, you understand the soul's need to free itself from all worldly burdens, all corporeal effects. To cast off the trappings that weigh upon the spirit's freedom.

Does that piece of white marble, with its delicate vein, hold some struggling spirit inside? Did I see the shape of its soul within the stone encasement? No. No I didn't. When my hand brushed over the surface, as I caressed its smooth and warm exterior and touched that slender vein, did I sense the flutter of a pulse? No.

Boris is right, I am no Michelangelo. To desire that marble is no more than an act of pride. Jack only bought that marble to get me working again. To inspire me while Premika's away. Okay... So *The Imaga Dea* will have to wait but the *Three Figures* could be finished. It could be fired and glazed before she gets back. Only the male figure is lacking.

I turn the small piece of paper over and over in my hand. The note, a flimsy jigsaw puzzle, is carefully reassembled. Under the tape and the tears is his name, Max. I look at his number. What to say when I call? *Hi, remember me?*

I dial the number, hoping that the right words will spring to mind when he picks up the phone. What if he doesn't remember me?

"Hello?"

"Hi, it's Alex. You might not remember me..." I start, then hesitate, a tad too long. Just hang up the phone. The male figure doesn't have to be him. It could be any man, that's the point. It could even be Jack.

"Well, perhaps if you gave me a hint," he suggests. The voice is playful.

"You were at my apartment a few months ago... you left your number and..."

He starts laughing. An easy, unselfconscious laugh. I relax a little.

"So which one are you?"

"The homely one," I say. "Listen, I know this sounds strange, but would you pose for me? I'm doing a piece and I really need your body."

Oh God, that didn't come out right.

"I mean, what I mean is, that I need a male body and I thought yours would do. Well, more than do, really..."

Max is laughing. He agrees to pose for me if I come to see him play.

"Play?" I ask. "What, hockey? Soccer? Chess?"

"Trumpet."

*****

I meet up with some acquaintances from my college days, post-modern-fringe-artist types, and we set off for the Bamboo Club on Queen Street West. We nurse fussy drinks and munch on chicken satays and coconut wrapped appetizers. We criticize the art on the walls but the comments spring from the jealousy that the work was someone else's.

"Boris is planning a new show," says a fellow artist, a woman whose work I never rated. "All sculpture. You should pop in and see him, Alex. You sculpt."

"He doesn't like my work," I say, shrugging off her suggestion. "He only likes crap."

"Well, he's showing me," says Peter, a guy I seemed to always compete with for bursaries and scholarships. "He's showing three pieces of my *crap*."

The night can only get worse unless I back-pedal. "Well, his taste must have improved then," I say.

The others buy it but it doesn't wash with Peter. He's in a snit. I am the enemy.

Finally the band arrives. Peter zeroes in on Max. His mood improves as he sets his sights on him. "He's dreamy. Wouldn't mind topping him."

I push my chair back. Lean on the two back legs, balancing. I keep quiet.

Max spots me in the crowd and smiles. He lifts his trumpet to his mouth, warming and moistening the cold metal cavity, darting his tongue in and out of the mouthpiece.

I right my chair. Stabilize it. Peter looks over at me, rolls his eyes. He gets the art show, but I'll have the trumpet player.

I get up from the table and I dance. I dance alone but I dance for him. He mutes his trumpet and watches me. Tonight we'll make love. He'll play me the way he plays his instrument. Rhythmically, melodiously, and just a little sadly.

*****

Max sits on his kitchen counter, barely fitting between the stove and the sink. His fingers are drumming on the stained arborite, as if keeping time with some inaudible band. I'm sipping a rather weak-but-not-helpless tea, while he slugs back his last beer. His hair, still damp from the performance, glistens off his face in a loose ponytail. There are curls at the temples.

"Must be hard making a living as a sculptor," he says.

"I cut headstones," I admit to my day job.

"Well, I'm glad you could tear yourself away from the graveyard."

"Me too."

Silence again, but for his digital thump, thump, thump. No words. We know where the night is heading, but neither of us know the way. I'm surprised he's so shy. I'm surprised that I am.

"You lied," he accuses.

"What?"

"You said you were the homely one." He swings his legs out and catches me between his thighs. Pulls me toward him. I reach up to the elastic band holding his hair in place and I pull on it slowly with my index finger until every strand is free. Loose about his neck and face. He looks at me through dark lashes and puts down his beer.

He leads me to his bedroom. Invites me to join him on his unmade bed. He is a vision, spread out on messy sheets, all long and muscular. The image of young masculinity touched with a hint of grace. I hadn't noticed how beautiful he was before. Hard to notice anything in Premika's presence. But now, here he is. It's just the two of us. No Premika. And he is every bit as lovely as I could imagine. His eyes are soft, almost sadly expressive, his face is lean and uncluttered, but it is his lips that are his defining feature. Full and inviting with an exaggerated swoop of his Cupid's bow. How to recreate what the years of practicing scales sculpted so diligently? How to echo the mark of his trumpet? I run my tongue over the surface of his swollen mouth, detailing the outline of the arc up and away from the opening, tracing the curve back down. I linger over the callous on the upper lip. Does he feel my licking, my biting, my teeth, my lips, my warm tongue?

65

Beneath me, he looks like the oil of *Eros*. My own Caravaggio of blood for paint. My knees grip him all the tighter for this. He is in my clutches, and yet not inside me. No. But my hand takes hold of him reverently. His head falls back, enraptured, enthralled. His eyes shut to the world. To me. The windows of his soul closed against me. What images crowd his mind as I move firmly over him with rhythmic intent? Does he imagine Premika is here with us?

No. No. She mustn't come into this. I must push her from my thoughts.

I refocus, concentrate only on him. From this incline, hovering in a straddle over him, it's difficult to tell from whom this sublime penis emanates. Max is so comely; his dark hair thrown back like *The Barberini Faun*. Bare-chested, almost hairless but for the few strays around his tight brown nipples. An unmapped terra-firma of chiseled flesh leading all the way down to the motion of my making. I touch myself as I move over him. My masturbatory crusade unites us. We are without gender. Without distinction. His sex is my sex. The stroking is my ecstasy as much as it is his. His orgasm belongs to me.

*****

Work on the *Three Figures* went easily after that night. With Max in my grasp, his body studied and remembered, my tactile memory was jogged. I set to work early on a Saturday morning and finished the sculpture before the start of my work week. Max didn't have to strip down to pose. Lovemaking was a study of his body, something I took from his bed and transported to my studio. The work was done quickly and I was pleased with the piece.

I stand in front of the kiln, waiting with Jack for the magic moment. The exact temperature of alchemy. How many times have we done this over the years? I look over to him. Jack, as ever, is too close to the door, feeling the heat from within.

"No air pockets?"

"No air pockets," I confirm.

It's a ritual. He asks every time because the first time I wasn't careful enough. The smallest air pocket caused the piece to blow up. Clay everywhere and everything in the kiln destroyed.

Jack views the piece to be fired. "You really push the limits, don't you?"

"What do you mean?"

"Well," he licks the sweat off his upper lip, "let's see, what have we got? Three nudes. This one appears to be you." He points at the figure that is me, "What was it, a ménage or something?"

"What makes you think that it wasn't imagined?"

"Come on. It's too good not to be true. Besides, you always do your research."

What difference does it make to the art how the piece is inspired? Enter the room in the *Uffizi* gallery where the paintings by Botticelli hang; do you stop to consider which were commissioned and which were painted from the artist's imagination? No.

"It's my take on the spiraling vortex."

"Well, if that's what you call it."

"A constant movement, no beginning and no end," I say, moving the piece gently so Jack can take in all sides.

"Must've been one helleva night." Jack steps back from the kiln. Just a footstep, but it's a sure sign that the temperature has hit at least 700 degrees Celsius. Two or three hundred more to go.

"It's an homage to *The Rape of the Sabine Woman*," I tell him.

"Well, maybe you should call it *The Rape of the Sabine Man,* although he doesn't seem to be struggling much."

"The Sabine men weren't raped. They were slaughtered."

"Well," he laughs, "I guess you got it wrong then."

Jack checks the thermometer. Along with my piece, Jack has a dozen large latte cups and saucers. His work, as a potter, is exact, clean and pleasing. His glazes are extraordinary. More delicate than Jack's gruff, working-class manner would suggest. He has always been a fan of Picasso's ceramics and the artist's influence is felt in Jack's finishing glazes. I once complimented Jack on his work and he shrugged it off. "They're just pots" he said. "Yeah, I'm a good *artisan.*" I have been cautious of complimenting him ever since. Now his pottery waits firing alongside my one piece. He seems so much more productive than I. But Jack does not rate his work. Even the most fragile, most exquisite ceramic he sees as no more than a pot. Only his large pieces, those huge pots with no possible use, only they give him any joy.

Jack walks around my clay work. "What was the last piece we fired? A goat giving head to a woman?"

"It was a satyr and a nymph."

"Still looked like she was getting head," he teased.

"Not sure that's the right term, Jack. I prefer cunnilingus myself."

"I bet you do. Hah!" Jack runs his rough fingers through his haphazard hair, "I noticed something about your work. I mean, if you don't mind me making an observation, that is."

I gesture for him to continue.

"It's sexual, but it's never loving or tender," he says.

"Tenderness and greatness don't go hand in hand," I counter.

"Oh yeah? What about the *Pieta* then?"

He's right, of course. The *Pieta* is great because it epitomizes tenderness. A mother holds her son in her arms. He is dead from the cross and limp in her sad embrace. But the heart-wrenching sorrow it evokes stems from the fact that Mary holds this grown man as though he were still her baby. We do not weep for the loss of a savior, but for the loss of a mother who holds the limp body of her dead son.

"The *Pieta* is great. But the tenderness is overwhelmed with sorrow."

"Well, it's not like you haven't had sorrow in your life. You should put your sorrow into that marble."

"Maybe I'm done with sorrow. I'm certainly sick of stone, working half my life with the likes of you, churning out generic headstones..."

"Memorials," he corrects. People who work in the death industry have adopted this new term to make the public feel more comfortable. We no longer say, *tombstones* or *headstones*. Even the term *marker* is frowned upon."

"Right. If they really were memorials, they wouldn't all look the same, would they? Headstones, tombstones. I'm sick of stone."

"You know what I think? I think you're scared. Clay is forgiving but marble isn't. You make a mistake with clay, you wet it down, reshape it. Poof, it's perfect again. But marble, fuck! You make a mistake and you've gotta chisel down a layer, create the image slightly smaller, all over again."

"It's not like I've never done a piece in marble. I did do a rather good male torso in marble once. Surely you remember?"

"That was a long time ago." His voice is flat. He remembers his discomfort, standing shirtless before me.

"I think you're the one who's scared."

Jack goes off to get a beer for himself. He uncaps the bottle on the side of his worktable. Looks at the *Three Figures* again.

"I guess I'm just too much of a pipe and slippers job myself. I had a girlfriend once who wanted a threesome. I was game at first because, you know, it's exciting. But then it just felt weird to me. Like there was nothing special between the two of us any more. It was all about sex and there was no love. Nothing tender, nothing sacred. Don't get me wrong, it was exciting. But nothing here," he says touching his heart. "It's all fun and exciting for you but all I see is a great talent going to waste. If I had your talent I wouldn't be wasting it on horny goats."

Was he joking? Surely even he could see the beauty of that piece. The satyr stretching, every muscle taut with the desire to please, as a perfect nymph of the forest takes time out from the hunt to balance expertly on his outstretched tongue. What an impossibility to design! The dimensions, the angles, the positioning -- all exact. That piece defied the nature of balance. It defied gravity. How could he stand there so smugly, calling it perverse? Besides, that piece garnered me the highest mark in my class!

"It's mythological, Jack," I correct.

"It may be that to you, but it's bestiality to me. All those stories you tell of swans making it with women, and bulls raping virgins. Just won't do here. Maybe that kind of thing is big in Greece or wherever, but for Chrissake, this is Toronto. You know what you need? A normal, down to earth relationship. Maybe a man this time?"

I don't tell him that I've just had a man. Max. The third figure in the piece Jack is firing. Down to earth, normal, or so it would seem. Perhaps Jack is right. Perhaps I should continue to see Max, even though I've finished the *Three Figures*.

"Not that *I'm* offering. I'm not your type. I've only got two legs after all."

"Satyrs only have two legs. It's centaurs that have four."

"Right, silly me."

"Stick your tongue out and I'll see if I can balance on it!" I laugh.

"Oh bugger off." Jack flips open the door. The heat pushes me back. Jack starts to feed the hungry fire.

*****

I start to unwrap *The Imaga Dea*. Take away the plastic wraps to expose her leathery, clay body. Is this her? Is this Premika? I look at her unfinished face, her head cocked to one side. This is all I've done. All I've completed and she hasn't returned. Hasn't contacted me. She was due back weeks ago. I want to slap her, make her feel what I feel.

"How could you!" I yell at the unfinished form.

She doesn't react. She just holds herself upright. She's so full of pride.

"I could destroy you if I wanted to." I run a hand over her shoulder, trace the fold of skin near her underarm. She is almost perfect, although she is unfinished. She is Premika remembered. And yet she is not quite exact. What makes her different? Her flesh is not warm. There is no blood beneath the surface of the clay. *The Imaga Dea* does not possess breath.

I stand on tippy-toes. Lean into my creation. I move my mouth near hers and gently exhale. My breath is a wish to create life, a life that will not betray me. But love me. Love me. Love me, as I love her.

Good God, I'm no better than Gepetto, doting over his wooden Pinocchio! Hoping that a blue fairy might let me wish upon a star. Or worse. But *The Imaga Dea* is not a Frankenstein or a Golem. Not a doll that comes to life at night. And she is not Galatia. She is an unfinished work. Nothing more, nothing less. Not Premika. Not a replacement.

I gather up the plastic. Yes, I will put her away for now. Get on with things. Jack's right, this isn't healthy. I need something more grounded. More real. I will push her from my mind as she has pushed me from hers. I must.

I place the first sheet of plastic on her torso and begin to wrap her like a mummy. I do not answer the phone when it rings, I just feed the wrap through my hands, circling *The Imaga Dea*. I hear my outgoing message making false promises that I will return calls. I pick up another sheet of plastic. Lay it over her perfect breasts. The answering machine beeps. I spritz the shoulders of *The Imaga Dea* but before I can cover her completely in plastic I hear a familiar voice.

"Hey, thought you needed my body. Call me. It's Max."

*****

I didn't allow Max into my studio the first few times he visited me. I wanted to keep him separate from my work. I tried to find a balance, to embrace something more tangible than my previous affairs. I thought it was time to experience something a little less obsessive. This meant that, although Max had a beautiful body and a natural grace, I could not coerce him to strip down and pose for me. I had learned my lesson. I would keep it separate, my work and my lovemaking. I also knew that if we had a chance at a relationship, I would eventually have to share that part of me that is the creator, the artist.

Max stands before the unfinished, carefully protected, object of my desire. She is safely covered in plastic, eager to be opened and admired. Max doesn't know this. All he sees is a shape, not quite my height, completely concealed by yards and yards of almost opaque plastic.

"What's under wraps?"

"It's unfinished." I'm unsure of what he'll think. Very difficult to reveal your work to someone after you've been intimate.

"Why the body bag?"

"She has to stay wet."

"Why?"

"Because," I pause, "she's not finished yet."

Slowly. I peel away the protective plastic wrappings, revealing my clay version of Premika. I undress her for my lover and watch him.

"It's got to be built up. It'll be larger, fuller when I'm finished. I'm calling her *The Imaga Dea*," I offer as a slight explanation, "The god in us that we project onto others."

Max looks at me blankly. He hasn't a clue.

"Or goddess in this case since she's, you know, female," I finish my thought.

"Very," mutters Max.

"Anyhow, she's not finished." I decide to spray her down since the wrappings are off her. Just to keep her moist. But then Max reaches for my hand and takes the water bottle from me.

"May I?" He starts spraying her body. Rivulets run between her breasts and gather in the indentation of her navel. He sprays her sculpted pubic bone and watches the droplets converge in her labial folds.

"It's your friend, isn't it? The one from the club that night."

I nod.

"She looks more beautiful than I remember."

"No," I contradict, "she's every bit as beautiful as this. It is a very close likeness. But it still needs to be detailed." I point to her clavicle, "You see? This isn't quite right. And the face doesn't have all her features yet. I've done all I can for now, worked from photos and prototypes. I will need Premika to finish it."

Max looks at me, furrows his brow, questioning.

"She's away. In Paris, modeling."

I reach for her wrapping. Suddenly I feel on shaky ground, worried that I could betray her, or myself. Or Max even. I gather up the extra hefty garbage bags and the yards of Saran wrap. Start pressing the moist plastic into her cracks and crevices.

"Hold on," Max says, "Just another minute or two." He walks all the way around her, taking her in one last time before she is mummified again.

"She's a bit sad though."

"Sad?" I ask, surprised that he should think that. She's indifferent, haughty, sexy and hungry. Ravenous to experience something greater than herself. But sad? Certainly sad is nothing I intended for her and certainly nothing I could see in her.

"I don't know," he tries to explain, but words are not his forté. "I don't know, I just see something kind of sad. Damaged, you know? I can't say why."

*****

I began to spend most weekends with Max. If he was playing a gig and I wasn't up to attending, I'd leave a key hidden near my door. Max would slip into my apartment, then slip into my bed. I enjoyed the heat of his body and the earthiness of his smell. His masculinity was as intoxicating as Premika's femininity once was.

Sometimes, during the most intimate moments, my mind would wander to her. I could be one with Max, physically joined, intent and focussed on him when suddenly I would imagine her in the room, watching our love making. My kissing would heat up, my movements intensify until Max would beg me, "Slow down, slow down. I don't want to come yet." But with the thought of Premika in the room, I became merciless, taking Max as my sexual prisoner all the way to his eventual release.

I often wondered if he shared the fantasy. We never discussed her. At least not in bed. But I did catch him once in my studio. He didn't ask permission to undress her. He peeled away the wrappings for himself. Stared at her naked body. Stood before her without moving. I thought I saw him whisper something and I felt a pang of jealousy. And when he finally saw me in the room watching him, he merely smiled and took me back to bed where he immediately fucked me without censure.

*****

Three nude figures, each looking at the other. Now fired, it has an earthier aura. It begs you to walk around it, look at it from above as well as below, discover how exactly the figures are joined. Touch it, turn it. Even Jack had to admit it's good, although not tender.

"What is this? Why are you standing around? Why aren't you working?" It was our task master, our boss, Amadeo. He rarely came into the work area, trusting the operations to Jack. But today, there he was. Present and curious.

He walks to the work table, peers over at the piece. I watch to see if he circles it, if I have truly cracked the spiraling vortex. Sure enough, Amadeo starts at the top of Premika's head, circles around the body which engulfs her, stands up and peers down at Max's masculine form and comes around to where Premika's body wraps from my own to touch Max.

"I get it! I get it!" He exclaims and he claps Jack on the shoulder. "Very clever, my boy!"

Jack starts to say that it isn't his work but Amadeo wags his finger at him, "No, no, I saw you carrying something in from your truck. You shouldn't be embarrassed. It's sexy but it is only natural."

Amadeo now places his hand on the fired clay. It rests on the figure that represents me. "Is this you, Alex? You modeled for Jack like this?"

"It isn't my work, it's hers," Jack nods toward me. "It's her work."

Amadeo turns and looks at me. Stares me in the eye, comprehending. He pulls his hand off the piece. Blows on his palm as if cooling the blisters of a sudden burn.

"You come to my office later. Now back to work!"

As Amadeo makes his way to the door, Jack leans over to me and whispers, "Looks like you made an impression."

*****

Amadeo didn't mention the small sculpture. He didn't question me on my inspiration; didn't ask why I would be moved to sculpt a study of three interconnected nudes. He just told me to sit and, after plunking an espresso in front of me, reached into his desk and pulled out a messy file folder. I opened it and entered a world I had never imagined. Before me were photos, all in black and white, of stone sculptures. Sculptures I was not familiar with, had never seen. I flipped though the images, beautiful, erotic and heart-wrenching, then stopped at an image so unlike the others that it caught my breath. Felt a tight and sad constriction in my heart.

The piece was a woman, young and round, with a child in her arms. The child's lips were parted and the woman was pressing her nipple to his mouth, urging him to suckle. By all reason it should not be a sad piece, and yet I was filled with a sorrow so inexplicable that I had to put down the file and compose myself.

"It is a memorial to my great-grandmother, she died giving birth to my grandfather. You see? It is a mother's love that goes beyond the grave. The breast he never suckled is offered from the other side. She mothers him from heaven. She feeds only his soul. He never knew her touch."

"And the others?" I asked.

"They keep her company," said Amadeo, pouring himself a hot cup of espresso. "You know, I used to go visit when I was a boy. Then one day my mother told me that we would be coming to Canada. I asked my uncle to take these pictures so I could remember my friends."

"Is that why you went into the memorial business?" I asked him.

"No. I told you already. It was my father's business. I inherited it. Now, my sons have no interest. One wants to be a doctor, the other one's in real estate. And my daughter? Well, this isn't woman's work."

I started to laugh, "No it isn't."

"No offense. You are an artist, not a woman."

I picked up the photos again. Extraordinary work, all unknown and on display for anyone strolling through the cemetery. There they were, outside, not stored away in a museum's basement, but in the open where someone, like the young Amadeo, could visit daily and become acquainted with their mystery.

"Now we just put up stones. Ugly stones. Same shapes, same words. No one wants to remember anybody anymore. Drink your coffee, it's getting cold."

I picked up the cup. Sipped.

"Some cemeteries don't even want stones. Just little plaques on the ground so they can cut the grass. Why can't they just go around?"

Amadeo was referring to the places that liked to call themselves parklands. A tranquil resting place in a park-like setting. The grass immaculately cut, green and weed-free with the consistent use of herbicides. You feel like you're walking across a golf course, not a sacred ground. Only when you look down at the small, discreet markers placed flatly into the lawn do you feel you are visiting the deceased.

"Pah! You know, Alex, you can tell a lot about people by the way they care for their dead," Amadeo paused, leaned across the expanse of his desk, "So. When I die, who's gonna take this business over?"

"I don't know," I said.

"What do you feel for Jack?"

I tried to race ahead, to puzzle together where this conversation might be going.

"Jack?" I asked.

"Yes. You love him?"

"Well, yes, he's my friend," I said, standing. I wanted to escape, return to the workroom.

"Hey, hey! Finish your coffee. The only thing I hate more than a lazy worker is a lazy worker who wastes my good coffee. My cousin sends it from Italy. You can't get good coffee here. You know who buys all the best beans?"

"The Italians?" I venture.

"Wrong. The Japanese, then the Germans then the Italians. It's true. We are number three when it comes to the beans. But we are number one at roasting. What we lack in the bean, we make up in technique. That, Alex, is the secret to everything."

*****

In the workroom Jack asks what Amadeo wanted.

"I don't know Jack. I really don't know," I sigh. "I guess he just wants me to work harder. Be a bit more punctual."

Jack laughs. We both know that I don't keep the hours that he and the others keep.

"It's a good job for you. You should try to keep him happy. Business is down. People are starting to get generic stones carved in China now. He doesn't want to lay anyone off but you never know."

I roll my eyes. If I didn't need the money. If I had other skills. If I were a known artist, working with architects, installing in front of important buildings and showcased in parks. If, if, if... I could outdo Kipling with my list of ifs.

"If you didn't have this job, what else could you possibly do?" he asks me. "You are pretty much un-hirable."

"Actually, there is one, " I tell him. "But I would have to live in England."

I proceed to tell him about a one time job at the Victoria and Albert Museum. Because early Victorian society decided that the penises on sculptures were immoral they smashed off the offending appendages. Greek gods and Roman heroes were defiled and emasculated. Their strength and beauty stripped from them in order to protect the eyes of the gentle Victorian viewer. But instead of tossing the many penises away, they were thrown inside a great, heavy chest. Unlabeled. Years and years passed and the penises were all but forgotten. Then someone discovered them and the museum decided that they should reassemble the marble. Now you wouldn't want to put the wrong penis on a statue, so someone, an expert, was hired to attach the appropriate penis on the correct stone body. He had to drill the injured marble and the severed penis, fit a metal peg between the two and then cement them together leaving no visible lines. I suppose after you'd reattached twenty or thirty penises you'd get bored though. And there were hundreds to do. But someone made a lifetime career of it.

"Well, I guess you're a closet *remasculator*," Jack jokes.

"Ah, it would have been the perfect job for me. But I was too young and came to sculpting too late, so I'm stuck here, cutting headstones."

My desire is not to cut memorials. Both Amadeo and Jack know this. They also know that there is no place in the work world for someone like me. And so they keep me, even if I am not as useful as some of the other workers.

I stay in for lunch and, when everyone else leaves the workroom, I go next door and sneak a peek at the uncut marble.

*****

I walk through St. James Cemetery on my way home. Wind my way through smallish headstones and larger family memorials. There is a peacefulness here. Large trees drown away the noise of the traffic and the lively sounds of the city beyond its wrought iron fence. It's hard to believe that people are rushing to health clubs or grabbing a quick bite at one of the many cafés or restaurants along Parliament Street. Oh, the face of Cabbagetown is changing. Soon the artists won't be able to afford it here. We will all be driven out. We'll find some other worn out area then, as we move in and bring it to life, others will follow, gentrifying to the point that we won't be able to afford it either. And the cycle will start again.

The cemetery is well kept, pretty. The gardens are properly tended. The walkways curve and meander past graves of past generations and graves yet to be filled.

Some of the headstones are so old that moss has crept over them and the writing has faded into the flat stone making the chiseled words hard to read. A child, not quite two, has a tired, flat marker that lifts from the earth at an angle. The words, *"Go gently, Mother Earth, on this child, who trod so lightly upon you."*

I read the words aloud, echoing them for my own mother perhaps. Guilty that there was no epitaph for her. No stone engraved. No memorial to mark her life. It comforts me to know that it was entirely her choice. Her wish was to be cremated and, for once, my father and I obeyed her wishes. When my father decided to start a new life, as he put it, he entrusted her ashes to me. I could have put her somewhere, placed her ashes in an urn on a shelf, or placed her inside a burial vault. But instead I freed her. It was the least I could do for her. I took her from the little box and threw her ashes into the wind. Watched as the little bits of my mother blew away from me.

From time to time a phrase moves me. A loss recorded on a memorial. A love remembered or regretted. But it's just words. There are no images here that move me. No statuary to speak of. An occasional angel with open wings, a cross, a large stone obelisk with a family name. But no nudes. And no mother with a baby suckling her breast.

There are great works of art in the cemeteries of Catholic Europe. Italy, France, Spain. The Père Lachaise Cemetery in Paris is certainly the most famous. At forty-four hectares, it is the largest park in Paris. But it is not the size of Père Lachaise that makes the cemetery famous. It is the art. Works were commissioned long before death as a way to demand respect. There are great works for names all but forgotten while simple monuments adorn some of the greatest heroes. These are the people who made Paris. The names of a culture. Voltaire, Heloise and Abélarde, Victor Hugo. Writers, lovers and artists stand equally beside politicians, businessmen and heroes.

The journalist, Victor Noire, rests at Père Lachaise. Bonaparte shot him because he disagreed with something Noire wrote. A rather severe critique of his writing! Over Noire's grave rests a bronze monument, a statue of him lying in repose. The piece excels in detail. The fabric of his clothes, the skin on his hands, his size, his shape, all exact. The artist took everything into account, even the detail of which trouser leg the journalist tucked himself into. Women began rubbing the bulge in his bronze trousers, hoping it could grant them fertility. Soon the patina began to change. It took on a shiny, glorious hue, which stood out from the rest of Noire's perfect body.

What do we have here, in Toronto, to compare with Noire's cock? Timothy Eaton's shoe. The large, patriarchal figure sits at the entranceway to the Eaton Centre, the mall which bears his name. His features, his face, his clothes have all taken on the dull patina of time. But his shoe, a shoe that is rubbed for luck countless times a day, shines like a beacon of hope. Here we worship at the foot of one of Toronto's wealthiest personalities while in Paris they worship at the groin of a murdered writer. Is it idolatry? Yes! But how wonderful to hope that the graven image of a dead artist, a magical bronze with a gleaming cock, might plant life in a yearning womb. Noire has a golden rod to set him apart from the many other bronzes and marbles. A shiny, golden rod, touched and rubbed and rubbed again. God, how jealous Bonaparte must be!

There are no bronzes with shiny penises in St. James Cemetery. No young women dancing with death, submitting to his seductive touch. No stones of passion, no heroic marbles. The grave sites are as dead as the bodies below them. Amadeo is right. Even death has become sanitized and commercialized. We can pay obeisance to Mammon, but we cannot worship fertility here. And we do not honour death. We do not offer it beauty. We do not create art in its name anymore. I would like to leave a bronze copy of my *Three Figures* here so that maybe, just maybe, a childless woman would pause to touch it, hoping that Max's cock would make her fertile.

*****

Max sits before the *Three Figures*, staring at it, saying nothing. I turn the piece, let him look at another angle. He shakes his head, gets up and walks from the room. From my bedroom, next door, I hear him open his trumpet case and begin the ritual of warming the mouthpiece. I wait to hear what sound he might produce, but I know somewhere, somehow, that he is disappointed.

A few notes, muddled and hastily blown and the trumpet is discarded. I wait, but Max doesn't emerge from the room, so I go to him, join him on the bed.

"You don't like it?" I ask.

"What I don't like," he says slowly, "is that you made it behind my back. I didn't pose for you. You asked me to pose for you but we never got around to it."

He expects some kind of explanation, but I am silent, not sure what to say.

"You took something that we did in private and you made it into something for everyone to see."

"Well, if it's any consolation, I didn't ask her permission either. She hasn't even seen the piece. Doesn't know it exists."

There. I said it! Brought her into the bedroom.

"But she posed for you. She posed for that other piece. So she knew you were..."

"What? Immortalizing her?" I cut him off. "So that one day, when her bones are nothing but dust and her actions are forgotten there will still be something of her left on this earth."

Max is quiet, pouting. His head is on my pillow, his hair is loose around his face, his shirt is riding up exposing the taut skin across his stomach. My eyes rest on that hollow that falls away from the hip. His V-line. A physical trait found only in lanky men. It's too easy to objectify Max, to focus on his body and ignore his feelings. Pout? What pout?

"You could be *The Barberini Faun*," I tell him and slowly begin unbuttoning his shirt.

"Are you going to show that piece?" he asks.

"Probably," I say, starting on the jeans. I push the top button through and then the other buttons pop open with the slightest pull. Beyond the coarse textured denim the first strands of his pubic hair curl up toward my hand.

"You're not listening to me," he accuses.

"I'm listening." My hand presses beyond the denim, encircles him.

"You don't fight fair," he yields.

"No," I say, coaxing his jeans off, peeling them away from his hips. He lifts to accommodate and I pull the fabric from his flesh until he is quite naked before me.

Max pulls me toward him, but I resist. I push him back onto the bed and step away. Yes, he could be the faun. The very piece that brought me to consciousness: sexually, creatively and imaginatively. How many times did my mind wander to the faun as my hands wandered over my own body? How many times had I been disappointed when a man disrobed and wasn't as perfect as him? Eventually I learned to separate my sexual expectations from my sexual desires.

I wasn't the first to lust after *The Barberini Faun*. Although it was the first image I lusted after. Greek and Roman sculptures were defaced and destroyed for their explicitness, but the faun was saved. It was kept in the clutches of the Vatican, away from the public in the Pope's private gallery. Centuries later European war and land disputes would divide the continent in a blood bath. The Pope told King Ludwig of Bavaria that he could have anything the church could provide if he cooperated in a land treaty.

"I'll have *The Faun*," he said.

"Anything but the faun," said the Pope.

But King Ludwig held out, even though the Pope tempted him with gold, jewels and wealth of all sorts. Eventually he left with *The Faun* and to this day he remains in Germany.

Except that his doppleganger lies on my bed. I part his thighs so they rest like the faun's, one leg off the bed, foot on the floor, the other knee bent up, foot resting on the covers. I prop up his torso, put pillows behind his back, then rotate his shoulders slightly. One arm dangles over the side of the bed.

"Don't move," I say. "Not an inch."

Max's ribs protrude through his taut skin, his muscles track between them. I lift his other arm, elbow pointing forward, forearm brushing past his ear, his cheek. I tilt his head to the right, and ease it back so that it appears that he has thrown it back in a moment's ecstasy, the curls unruly, falling away from his brow. My finger tips close his eyes.

Perfect. Almost perfect. *The Barberini Faun* is unlike other masculine statuary because he is spent, the ecstasy is past and he lies back in an afterglow. *The Faun* has already been ravished, has given himself over to the lover. Has been submissive, allowed himself to be receptive, enraptured and willfully violated.

Max is aroused. I drop between his splayed legs, rub my cheek lightly against his inner thighs as my hands press upon his knees forcing them wider. I breathe over his skin, my mouth making its way to his cock. Lips barely parted I explore its length, make my way to the tip. Max sighs in anticipation. He reaches for my head, tries to stroke my hair but I push him back down into position, then take him into my mouth.

Don't speak. Don't ruin this image with your voice. Become the Faun, give me that fantasy.

Max moans. I grip his thighs more tightly. Then I tease. My teeth gently, barely, touch his skin. I move up and down him until he's impatient. Tortured from the ceaseless tease. I oblige him now. Apply more force until my lips are numb, my mouth is tired, and my tongue tastes his pleasure.

On my bed is *The Barberini Faun*. Drained, depleted and supine. He slowly opens his eyes, looks at me. Takes his arm from behind his head and reaches a hand to me. I join him on the bed. No point in making him hold the position, the image has already been preserved. By someone else.

"Thanks," he says, wrapping an arm around me so my head rests on his shoulder.

"Thank you," I whisper back and Max softly laughs. He doesn't know the relief I feel knowing that I can enjoy his body without feeling the need to capture his soul.

Later Max plays his trumpet. It's unlike anything I've ever heard him play. I ask him where he learned it and he tells me he was just riffing on a theme. I urge him to write it down and he shrugs off the suggestion.

"I live in the moment. Music is improvisational for me."

The notes float away, lost forever. Intangible.

*****

It was Max who encouraged me to bring the three figures to Boris. I'd told him that Boris was doing a sculpture exhibit and, because he didn't know Boris, he thought that Boris would be impressed enough to show the piece. I was surprised at how insistent Max was considering how pissy he had been when he first saw the *Three Figures*. I suppose that although his pride was hurt his ego was complimented.

Boris picks up my portfolio and begins to look through photos of my other works. He still hasn't taken in the *Three Figures*.

"I need to show, to build my résumé to the point where I might qualify for a grant from one of the arts councils."

"You want a grant? Why? Do you need the money or does your ego need the approval of some jury of supposed peers?"

Boris flips through a few pages, scans some photos of work he hasn't seen before. "You know, I am a fan of yours. You have great ability. That is a big compliment from me. But, tell me, what goes on here?" he taps his forehead. "Is there a thought in your head? An opinion perhaps? What do you have to say? How will your art possibly make this world a better place?"

"Boris, tell me, how do your gruesome images make the world a better place?"

Boris leans back on his chair, balances on two legs. I hate it when he does that. It is a gesture that signals that I am under his scrutiny.

"But at least I have something to say about the world around me. At least I am aware that there is a world around me. Too much introspection hurts an artist."

"Actually, you think that you are holding up the mirror of truth, showing the world how ugly it has become. But all you're really doing is adding more ugliness to it. Do you really think that showing the very worst of humanity will be a wake up call? The public will snap out of its complacent stupor because someone happened to come by your little gallery?"

Boris returns his chair to its four legs. I suppress a smile.

"Touché," he chuckles. "I've missed our little talks. You keep me on my toes. You're my great accuser, my own personal Satan."

"I can't possibly accept that role," I reply.

"I mean it in the kindest way."

"Yes, but if I were your personal Satan, then I'd have to acknowledge you as God."

Boris starts to laugh. Then he turns my book towards me and points at the *Three Figures*.

"Want to tell me about this piece then?"

"It's called *Three Figures*. It's a tribute to Giovanni Bologna."

"I can see that much. Here I see you, not terribly flattering I must say. And here is Premika, of course. Still your great muse I see. Then we have some poor innocent man you've seduced together. Does he actually exist or is it a fantasy you share. It could have been me I suppose, but I mustn't flatter myself."

I do not tell Boris about Max. Better he think him a fantasy, that the flesh and blood man does not exist. I do not tell him that Max often waits for me in my apartment. That he satisfies me. Helps me forget the woman who has left us both.

"It's interesting," says Boris. "You see how you and the young man are focussed on her? Although she offers you her face to kiss and she offers him her cunt to fuck, she really isn't interested in either of you, is she?"

Boris hands me back my portfolio. "The documentation of your sexual conquests are always of interest to me. But they would not speak to someone you haven't bedded. Although, I suspect your audience is growing by leaps and bounds."

"So you won't show me then."

"I didn't say that. Right now I don't think your pieces will work with the other sculpture I'm showing, but give me some time to think about it. Maybe I will come by your place and see the original."

No. He mustn't. Not with *The Imaga Dea* taking up a corner of the room, under wraps. I stand, reach for my jacket. Prepare to leave.

"If it's money you need, I may be able to get you a commission."

"Really?"

"We'll see. Leave me a few photos. And don't be such a stranger. You know my door is always open to you."

"Thanks."

"You know, I'm still waiting for that one great piece."

"Which one is that?" I shift my weight. Take a step closer to the exit.

"You know. The one that answers my mandate."

There is no pretending now. The bet is still on. Why do I need to prove myself to Boris?

"She's in Paris," I blurt out.

"Really? Paris?" he asks. "I thought she was afraid to fly."

I leave the gallery. I start walking. Walking and walking. As far away from Boris as I can get. Three blocks from the gallery, I feel like crying. I try blinking, but I lose the battle and must wipe at my eyes. Why am I crying?

I sniffle back the pathetic proof of my self pity and hurry on toward the subway then down, down the steps away from the assault of the mockingly cheerful sun. Persephone, stealing herself away from the harsh glare of the world, underground. Into the comforting dark world of Hades, where Boris dares not go.

Is there a thought in your head?... He dared to ask me that? How many times have I wished my brain could be liposuctioned so that I could be free of my excess thoughts! How freeing it would be to think less and to live more in the moment. Like Max. Happy to play a little tune, to improvise something new, then smile benignly as the sounds slip away into oblivion. Happy, no *content*, with all things ephemeral and fleeting.

People look away from me. They look away from the crying woman. It's embarrassing. Awkward. Real. Better to stare at the billboards with their airbrushed advertisements. The woman must be mad, weeping in public, eyes welling up beyond control. That's what they think when they see me.

But my mother never thought that. She thought it mad *not* to cry. *There, there now. Let it go, that's right Lexie. Let it go.* And somehow, small in her arms, the pain would go with every tear. As if by draining the excess water the troubles would flow away too. And there, small in her arms, I would know contentment, comfort. What comfort did I bring her in the end? None. Why, why is that? Because I felt that if I didn't witness the dying that perhaps her death wouldn't come. So I raced against time, tried to create something that would give her joy. Something that would make her see me a s a success. Something that would give her life. I worked endlessly on a small marble bust of her. Wanting to give it to her before she died. But I didn't finish it in time. I failed. And I haven't created anything in marble since.

"See me, see me? I've failed. This is the face of failure," I want to yell out to the random strangers I pass. Now that would be performance art fitting enough for Boris and his stupid mandate! A commission perhaps, but never a show. Well he isn't the only gallery owner in Toronto!

I wait for a red subway. I stand behind the yellow safety-line, close to the mouth of the tunnel. Beyond the tunnel the tracks veer sharply to the right. I know this, even though the bend is beyond my blurry field of vision. What I can't know is the colour of train. Not until it rushes from the tunnel and slows to a stop in front of me. I look down at my toes. They barely touch that yellow safety-line. How tempting to take a step and be free of criticism.

Boris wants that piece. *The Imaga Dea.* He wants nothing less. But I cannot give it to him because she is still away. And so I wait. I wait. And with every day I become a bit more invisible. To the world. To her. To everyone but Max.

*****

Then it happened. She returned. Breezed carelessly back into my world.

Max and I sit at the bar, checking out a band his friends are in. I'm still on edge because I hadn't wanted to go and he begrudged having to persuade me. He's on his third beer, from the bottle, while I nurse a vodka tonic. The music is too loud, I'm tired and Max seems far away. I don't attempt to bridge the void, I'm still pissed that he introduced me to his friends as a graveyard worker. I lift the lemon wedge from the glass rim and bite into its unbearable tartness. Max drums his fingers on the table. I cross, then uncross my legs. And see her.

Most people attempt suicide as a way of reaching out for help. Because they can't vocalize their need, they speak through actions. Some say it's brave to commit suicide. Some say it's cowardly. To me, it's just checking out.

I leave the bar without speaking to her. Run blindly into the night. To stay would be, what? Did she know I was there? I don't know and I would never ask her.

Max arrives home angry and drunk. My leaving was a personal affront.

"No, no!" I say, showering him with misplaced kisses.

He reaches beneath my skirt and tears down my white cotton panties. Ah, just take me. Make me feel wanted. Make me forget.

He turns me away from him. Plasters me against the wall. His breath is behind me, close to my ear. Hot with alcohol. I close my eyes, see her face. It couldn't be her. Just someone like her. But this. This is immediate. His hands grabbing. Clutching. Separating. His finger probes, explores and tests the boundaries of my tolerance. I tell him "no," but he's breathing "yes" into my ear. Unmuted, finally, he sounds his will. Stabs at me, searching for the place to give way to his voice.

In the darkness of the bar he had seen her. Followed the path of my gaze and in that moment realized the duplicity in my heart. Now if only I could lie, tell him that she means nothing really. Give him, at least, that. But my hand covers my mouth. I bite through the skin as he penetrates me. In a lover's moment of synchronicity we break flesh together.

There is blood on my hand.

CHAPTER 6

I stand in my usual spot. The billboard across from me has been replaced. No longer Aphrodite with her bottle of Infinity. Now there is a younger, paler, fresher face. More accessible. Less exotic. She has been replaced. But not for me.

It has been over two weeks since I spied Premika in the bar. Two weeks, and she hasn't contacted me. I have been worse than replaced. I have been discarded. I am the forgotten one, not her. I am *L' Inconnue*.

L'Inconnue. The unknown one. The forgotten woman. A face that inspired a thousand death masks. But nobody knew who she was. Even Boris had a first run copy of the mask. I remember lying on his bed, my head propped up on goose down pillows, staring at the mask on the opposite wall. About the same distance from me as Premika's replacement billboard is now.

"Who is she?" I asked him.

"A modern Ophelia. Post romantic. Drowned in the Seine. Quite common at that time."

"Death masks or drowning?"

"Both."

Boris had a habit of ending a conversation by answering with a one word explanation. But I was on to him. I pressed my body into his, breathed my words into his ear.

"You know so much Boris..."

And he knew that if we were going to go a second round he would have to tell the story and possibly reveal just a little of himself to me as well. He wrapped his arms around my body, prevented me from moving away and I knew that I would win his story and pay for it later.

"She was sold to *La Morgue*. Nobody identified the woman's body and nobody went to the *gens d'armes* looking for a missing woman. So they made a death mask of her face before she started to decompose. Nobody recognized the mask. People began saying that she was a mermaid dredged up in a fisherman's net. So... An artist understood the power of her beauty and saw that with her mystery and her face he could turn a nice profit. He made copies of her death mask. People found it all very romantic. Tragically beautiful. Even my wife was moved by the story. She choreographed a modern ballet about it. The fisherman pulling the body from the water; the woman, dancing her story with a certain madness, but as a phantom because she's already dead of course." Boris laughs. "My wife excelled at madness and death. The dance of the unknown made her quite well known in the dance world. I surprised her and gave her the mask opening night."

"Your wife?" I asked. It was the first he had mentioned her.

"Ah, yes. Such is the irony. The mask of the unknown woman remains. But the whereabouts of my wife remains unknown."

"You don't know where your wife is?"

"Well, not quite true. She is in Europe. Stuttgart perhaps."

We never mentioned his wife again and the next time I visited him I noticed that the mask had been replaced by a small bas-relief I had done in someone else's class. It was a self portrait. I didn't ask him why he had it or why he hung it on his wall. But now, now that I am no longer his flavor of the month, I cannot help but wonder if that too has also been replaced.

A red train stops. It is heading in the wrong direction. Away from my apartment and towards downtown. Towards Bay and Bloor. Towards Premika's condo. I am tempted to jump onboard and just show up. Buzz her apartment and force myself back into her life. But how?

The train passes. I get onto a silver one going the opposite direction.

*****

I'm wedging clay in my studio. The piano wire slices through another lot. Cleanly dissecting, separating into two. An occasional breeze makes a hasty tour through the studio, touching me without commitment before it wafts away through the open door that leads to my small deck.

Why hasn't she phoned me?

I grab up some more clay, escape into the work at hand. This I understand. There is no mystery here, no hidden agenda in clay. Here empty spaces are beaten into non-existence. I extend the width between my opposing fingers. An extra two inches is all. My hands feel strong, and I knead. It resists me, I press harder. If there is too much clay, if I've taken on too much, I'll keep wedging. Removing air pockets.

I start the process of throwing the clay down. Hurling it over and over again onto the prepared surface. It absorbs the wet. Sucks out the villainous spaces. Each time I break down its resistance. Each time I remove another air pocket.

I want only substance now. It's physical work, I can smell my efforts. I wipe wisps from my eyes, away from a damp forehead. Should have cleaned the clay from my hands first. It doesn't matter, there's no-one to see me.

Maybe it wasn't her in the club that night. Maybe my eyes deceived me because I wanted it to be her. But then there was that photo in *Now Magazine*. A new club opened on Queen Street and all those edgy types were there. The hip, the beautiful, those on the fringe of every art scene. And there she was, her unmistakable profile, in black and white newspaper print. When was that? Days ago? A week? Forever?

Take a moment before continuing. I sip my cold coffee. It's been in my mug for hours, the milk lifting away, separating to the surface. It's bitter now, stale. The fragrance gone. Funny, it was so inviting earlier. No matter. Soon the caffeine of life will flow through my numbed veins. Keep me going. I will finish this piece. Complete *The Imaga Dea* with or without her. I could have been working on it all along, after all my fingers know her. I don't need her here to pose. I don't need her for inspiration. I don't need her at all!

My fingers tug at my sticking t-shirt, leaving streaks of clay at the neckline. One more sip of life's essential poison, then back to work. Lifting handfuls to the wire. Slicing. Pounding, kneading and absorbing. Again and again and again. No air pockets now. Only substance, pliable and yielding.

Then I hear something. The creak of a floorboard. A footstep. I reel around startled.

"You're a sight for sore eyes," she says nonchalantly. It irritates me. I'm pissed and cranky. She could have called sooner. Could have sent a post card from Paris. Could have done something, anything, but suddenly it doesn't matter. She's beside me, her scent in my nostrils. Her palms on my face persuading my gaze to meet hers.

"Did you miss me at all?" she teases.

"No. Not at all," I reply

*****

All other works have been put away. Anything completed is stored in Jack's warehouse, including all the earlier maquettes as well as the *Three Figures*. The entire room has been devoted to her and only her. Today we will finish the piece.

It's a hot and sticky afternoon. We're sculpting, or rather I'm sculpting her. Have been at it all morning without a break.

"What happened with your father?" I ask her.

Premika shrugs. Waves her hand with a dismissive gesture. She stays naked. Open. She is still lying back but that look of ecstasy now has a twisted tinge of regret.

"Stay just like that," I order her.

I wet my hands. I touch the clay brow, add an arched furrow. Slide my muddied hands to her shoulder and, with direct force, I dislocate the joint. I feel her break in my hands. Then softly and gently I smooth over the wound, rework the clay to fill and shape her arm and shoulder until finally her gesture is filled with ambivalent dismissal.

"So?" I ask.

Premika sighs.

"I wanted to meet him. So I forced the issue. Demanded that he acknowledge me. But he kept finding excuses. Finally he told me that he had never told his wife about my Mom. Never said that he had a daughter. He said I would muck up his life. I was nothing more than a mistake to him. An inconvenience. His children in India were more important."

She tells me fragments, on and off. But it is a childhood hurt. And childhood hurts never go away. They imprint too deeply on our nascent hearts, our tender flesh, our trusting minds. They form us. Every betrayal, every pain, every loss is a blow of the sculptor's chisel, until we are shaped and formed into the person we ultimately become. Premika pulls her knees into her chest and rests her forehead on them.

"Sometimes I dream of becoming so famous that even he will have to look at me. See me everyday, as a reminder of what he rejected. Sometimes I dream that I do something so special it makes all the news everywhere in the world and he can't brag that I'm his daughter because he never acknowledged me. I thought modeling could make me famous, but it's too trivial."

Premika stretches her body and shakes the stiffness from her limbs. I hand her a robe and she ties her sash loosely around her waist. She's tired. We both are.

"Good work," I say. "Your part is done."

This is it. She will never have to be naked before me again. Never have to strip down. The time has passed. The piece is complete. Perhaps now we can both feel resolved. But all I can feel are the folds of the dark blanket wrapping around me and the emptying of my inner being.

She walks over to the front of the piece and stares at it. I watch from behind her. See her shoulders move subtly. Then I hear the sounds of gentle sobs. Little breaths and gasps.

"What? What?"

She shakes her head.

"Why are you crying? Don't cry. It was supposed to make you happy, not upset you."

Now she's sobbing. Sobbing. And I don't know what I can do. All I do know is that, try as I might, I still love her and it kills me to see her so distraught. I do not want her to have a pain I can neither understand nor alleviate.

"She'll never change. She'll never age. She'll never be replaced or rejected."

"No. You are frozen in time. A moment preserved."

Premika turns to me. She pulls her robe snugly to her body and wipes her face with her sleeve. "I'm sorry, I'm overtired. I gotta go."

But she doesn't move. She just stands in front of her image, tears streaming over her lightly rouged cheeks.

"Premika, Premika," I say. I take her in my arms and press my cheek to hers. "You're perfect Premika, I sculpted you exactly as I see you."

Then her mouth is pressed to mine. Her tears and snot run onto my face but I don't care. *Please God, please, let me have this moment. Make it last. If it lasts I will somehow find my faith in you.* But why should *He* listen to me? I haven't shaken hands with the invisible god. I've only shook my fist at Him and challenged His ability to create.

She steps back, composes herself. She's Premika again. Full of confidence and in control.

"Well, I guess you've won your bet with Boris then. What was the wager?"

I look at her in amazement. How could she know about the bet?

"There was no wager. Only the bet. Well more like a dare really. No, more of a challenge really."

She gathers up her discarded clothes and goes into the washroom to change. Closing the door between us.

The Imaga Dea looks amused. Premika's tears haven't affected her in the least. She is frozen in her rapture, unaware of the emotion she has evoked. I'd love to keep her just like this. Free of scars and marks. Flawless. But gods are born again and again. They endure so many deaths. A needle pricks the thigh. A heart is crushed into pomegranate seeds. And a crown rests immortal in the sky.

To immortalize *The Imaga Dea*, to place her amongst the stars, I must first pierce her with a knife. Cut her. Scar her and break her before I leave her to be eaten by flames.

I pick up my sculptor's knife, touch my finger to the blade, until a small bead of blood forms on my fingertip. This is how it will feel. I press a little harder until my blood runs the length of my finger and onto my hand. Then I turn my attention to her. I place my mouth next to her ear, whisper, "You'll never believe how sorry I am. You'll just never know."

But it's too soon. She isn't ready. She has to harden. Toughen up a bit.

"Forgive me," I say to her. But somehow she has lost her innocence.

Before Premika returns, I go to the kitchen and wash the blood from my hands.

*****

After hours. Premika's taken me to an underground booze can she sometimes frequents. A leftover from the Festival of Festivals where blurry eyed filmgoers could grab a drink before starting the marathon all over again. When the festival ended this one remained and, when armed with the right password, its cavernous interiors opened to the knowing nocturnal clubber.

Premika's dancing alone in a corner while I argue with some drunk pseudo-intellectual about socialism in the free world. A blur of smoke, vodka and unformed thoughts. This is her world. A world that is far, far away from my studio. A world that no longer intrigues me.

Across from me are two guys chopping a line with a credit card. One rolls up a twenty and catches my eye. He smiles and indicates that he'd share. I shake my head, look away from him. Scan the room.

Premika's laughing with someone in a corner. Her head's thrown back, swan-necked. And a man is smiling. He's well dressed for this place. Silk shirt, Italian trousers, and his shoes are the same colour as his burgundy tie which hangs loosely from his bull-like neck. So unlike the others in this smoke filled room. He leans into her, whispers something and she laughs a little harder.

My free-world socialist loses steam through the cracks of my attention span. His gaze relocates to the silhouette of a stoned brunette, and he slips away. I'm relieved. Enough talk. Not words. An act. Time to dance.

I'm aware of my body. Awkward. Conscious of every move. Of being watched. It's always that way at first. Then this other being steps in, tenacious with animal preservation. Claiming my body, bending and gyrating it. Marking the floor as mine. The dancing changes to calculated abandon. Like a controlled orgasm. I reach an apex I can sustain for hours. A heightened pitch. Now I don't care if I'm being watched. My ego escapes into the ephemera. I'm soaring. Lost. To the world, to the people around me, and lost to Premika.

A guy makes his move, "Wanna dance?"

"I am already." Rather obvious, I should think. I own the floor.

But he won't be put off, "So, you having fun?"

"Uh huh," I reply. "In a George Sanders kind of way."

Some say it's brave to commit suicide. Some say it's cowardly. George Sanders left a note saying he was leaving this world because he was bored.

The guy moves on, clears my path of vision. I catch sight of Premika leaving with the man, his fingers curling around the belt loops of her jeans. I dance through the next hour, then I go home. Alone.

*****

I can't sleep. The sloping ceilings of my apartment press down upon me. The window is open but only street noises drift in. How can there be people on the street? Going to work, or going to bed? Girlish coy laughter.

I can't sleep. Fingers move along the rib cage, then down. Down the stomach. Poised, well trained in the art of self satisfaction. It will help me sleep. Oblivion.

Premika is making love to him. She left without a good-bye and now he is in her bed. Will he simply come and go? Or will he spend the night? No, no. I know Premika. Sleeping is far too intimate.

A hand to my lips, my mouth. I can taste expectation at my finger tips. Now they trail over the throat. Across the breasts and belly. Along the hipbone. Grazing the skin lightly. Barely touching. Wait... Wait... Softly. Softly circling. Slowly, slowly separating.

My ego, escaping. I'm soaring. Almost lost. Except that I keep thinking of her leaving with that man. His hand securely in the hollow of her back. His fingers curling around a belt loop.

An accommodating stretch. Easier to reach. Vulnerable. No surprises, the comfort of old routine. The pinching of skin, the puckering of a nipple, the hardening of experience. The tease of predictable touch.

His hot breath moving over her, caressing her breasts, kissing her. Hungering down to sample her soft, salty sweetness. Drinking her in.

I shudder violently and weep in the empty odour of myself. The French call orgasm *La petite mort.* Perhaps suicide and masturbation are not unalike.

****

I'm dreaming of a warmer place. There are streams of sunlight across a turquoise sea. I'm on the shore sculpting a large piece. Cutting through marble.

A man approaches, his dark hair blowing in the ocean air. His skin is sun-kissed and moist.

"What are you sculpting?" He asks.

"Symposium," I tell him. *The answer surprises me. There is only one figure before me and not two disjointed lovers struck asunder by jealous gods.*

"How can you possibly?"

He looks like Max, but sounds like Boris. Either way, he knows. They both know that I'm an impostor. I look into the man's face. Max's face. Boris's voice.

I'm in the ocean now. Struggling. Trying to keep my head above water. It changes from turquoise to red. Menstrual red. The waves are turbulent, crashing over my head. Suddenly the water parts and a Rodinesque figure emerges. It's Premika. Posing. Balancing one foot on the tangible rock and one on the capricious water. Aphrodite rising out of the sea foam. Her perfume ad.

I try to swim over to her. She reaches to me and scoops me up. Takes me. Reunites me with my perfect half. I cling, arms round her. Blood-red water drips from my body onto hers. I'm here. I'm here. Kissing her salt skin. Having her. Let all the gods be jealous!

But her body turns stone cold and her warm soft folds of skin harden into form. Premika is gone. Forever lost. Only The Imaga Dea remains.

*****

I have reached inside her. Her innards are piled on the studio floor. Traces of her are stuck to my hands and wedged under my nails. She is disemboweled and eviscerated. A shell.

If the shell is beautiful enough, one never considers the creature inside. Lovers, children and dreamers on vacation collect shells on the beach as mementos of what? Carefree times? Holidays? Sunny skies and shimmering seascapes? It's never as a reminder of the previous tenant. A fleshy mollusk, an invertebrate. A spineless creature.

She's a beautiful shell, *The Imaga Dea*. A leathery, earthy damp exterior, and wholly hollow inside. A shell, a reminder of vacations gone by. She's the light streaming into the studio, an afternoon of secrets, and the smell of Premika. They say that if you put your ear to a seashell you can hear the ocean. If I put my ear to the empty *Imaga Dea* will I hear the hollow echo of her laughter? Will I hear the sound of drops, tears she cried over growing old?

Nothing. Not a sound. Silence, but for the point of a blade piercing three imperceptible holes in the shell of her body. Her nipples, her navel - escape routes of breath.

What would Premika think of this hollow, spineless creature?

Slowly the intense Malone-red of her thighs and back will dry and pale. Her breasts will become more flesh-like, her belly more human. As the clay readies itself for the flame, *The Imaga Dea* will become less god-like, more mortal. She will acquire a new beauty in her vulnerability.

*****

We sit at a booth in the Avenue Road Diner. The light seems harsh, unforgiving in these window seats. Premika needn't fear the light though. She has a light gloss on her lips, a faint blush brushed across her cheekbone and a flick of mascara darkening her thick lashes. I, on the other hand, am not prepared for the light of day. My hair is not a shiny mane; it is barely brushed. I look pale, almost anaemic in this northern light. But Premika always looks sun-kissed.

"Someone may join us," Premika informs me.

"Oh?"

As I sip my cappuccino I silently wish that her guest won't show. I want to keep what time we have for us alone. Why must she bring a third party into it?

"I may have a commission. Boris mentioned something."

"Oh?" She couldn't sound more bored.

I look out the window in time to see a man hurrying to the door. It's him. The man from the booze can. He enters with all the self assurance of a diplomat and sits with an air of ownership. Premika leans her face toward him and he kisses her with a certain familiarity. Then with a flawless smile he turns to me and offers his hand in greeting.

"Hi, I'm Victor," he says in a plummy voice, almost British.

"Alexandra. Well, Alex. Or Lexie, whichever you prefer."

He laughs. He actually seems to like me.

"You're a painter?"

"Excuse me?"

Victor points at my jeans. There are paint splotches and a few smears of clay. I had just finished hollowing out *The Imaga Dea* and, because I was running late, hadn't changed out of my work clothes.

"No," I reply.

"It's too bad, I was looking for someone to paint my new condo," he laughs. "Wait till you see it Premika. Exposed brick walls, high ceilings. Retro and modern at the same time."

I look down at what I'm wearing. Rub the back of my hand against the offending stains.

"I'm an artist."

He's lost interest, after all, he needs his place painted. He snatches up a menu. "So tell me, what's good here?"

Premika signals for more coffee. I lift my cup for a refill. I shouldn't though, I'm antsy enough as it is.

"So how do you know Premika?"

Deeply, I want to say. I know her intimately. I know her in ways you cannot imagine.

"Alex is the one who's sculpted me," she explains, although it sounds more like a reminder.

"Really?"

"It's a life size piece. In clay though."

"I'm rather fond of clay," I interject.

Victor closes the menu. He's made his choice.

"You want me to buy it for you?"

"Why would you buy it, you haven't seen it?" I ask him.

"Well, if it looks like Premika, it must be beautiful."

Premika smiles at him and he leans over to her and kisses her temple. I feel sick.

A waiter comes to take orders. Victor's having a breakfast of champions. Eggs, sausages, toast, the works. I'm no longer hungry. I stick with my usual sticky bun.

I watch as Victor works through his food, devouring sausages and dunking crusts into the runny centers of his eggs.

"Victor is from Calcutta," Premika announces.

"Really? You don't look Indian," I blurt out. How tactless. How politically incorrect. But there it was.

"I'm Anglo-Indian. There are a lot of us out there." He takes Premika's hand.

"Oh, and I thought you were exotic!" Premika jokes.

"I am truly exotic!" He responds.

Is that the attraction? Something familiar from the land of her father? He is handsome, I have to admit. But not my sort. Too manicured, too predictable. And he sounds like a 1930's film actor. There is money there. He smells of it. Leather and success. Handsome, successful, relaxed. How could she be attracted to that?

I get up to leave. Make for my wallet but he gestures that he will pay.

"Going so soon?" Premika asks.

"Yes. I got a hot date."

*****

"Hot as Hell in there already. Won't be long now." Jack pulls an old rag from his back pocket and wipes his forehead. He may be sweaty, dirty and unkempt, but he is - and I suppose always will be - the keeper of the kiln. A Virgil at the gate, inviting one to the fire. In a moment he'll open the door, lay wide the gates of Hell. The inferno will blaze, hungry with licking flames, tongues of heat. And we will feed her to the kiln, assured that she has the spirit to survive. Will this flaming Hell transform her?

Jack checks the thermometer then looks at his watch. He's not in a hurry. Jack's never in a hurry. He's just measuring the climb of the mercury with the ticking of his watch. 900, 950, 999 degrees celsius. Tick, tick, tick, soon. How hot does Hell get?

In the third ring of the seventh circle of Hell, grows a dense and unwieldy forest. Every tree embraces the soul of a suicide. A soul imprisoned for all of eternity in bark and branches and twigs. Razor-clawed harpies nest amongst the souls, amongst the trees, picking at the leaves. The suicide's soul bleeds, cries.

"Hot enough now."

And the gates of Hell fly open. The heat throws me back. Jack struggles with a piece.

"She just fits." He closes the door and flips the lock. She's inside now, gestating, transforming. Suffocating in the heat. Over 999 degrees Celsius for eight hours, maybe more, as the mercury climbs higher still.

"Hey, you wanna beer?" Jack asks. He's no longer my Virgil at the gates of Hell, just a guy I've known forever. That's the magic of Jack. He shape shifts with ease, without thought. I trust *The Imaga Dea* to him and his alchemy. I trust him.

"So, are you over her now?" he asks.

"Over whom?"

He nods toward the kiln. I wonder how she's faring inside.

"I don't know. Maybe I'm incapable of love."

"You're capable of it. That's why you avoid it. You'd rather be obsessed than committed. You're afraid that love would take up too much time. You think you need freedom to sculpt."

He could be right. Do I know the difference between obsession and love? Is there a difference? We all accept love as a given right while obsession's been maligned, given a bad rap. *You don't love her, you're merely obsessed.* And as love is raised up as the ideal, obsession is sneered at as unhealthy, damaging and destructive. But what movements have begun, what discoveries unearthed, what masterpieces created if not for obsession? It is desire that breeds a restless heart. Desire that leads to obsession. And once that obsession consumes you, once you can no longer just think or dream of that obsession, then, and only then, do you pick up your pen, grasp your chisel, or clutch your paintbrush. It is then that you create.

But for love you must sacrifice. You compromise. I watched my mother put away her dreams, first for my father and then for me, until she was without an identity, without an ego. A shell. By the time the cancer raged through her bones, there was nothing left for it to devour. My father and I had already eaten her alive.

"A therapist once told me that I make myself a victim of a rotating muse."

Jack laughs. Caught off guard, a spray of beer escapes his mouth.

"It's true. Some men are victims of sequential monogamy. Instead of taking a mistress they feel they have to divorce and marry the next woman who comes along. I do the same thing, except I replace one inspiration with another."

"You think it's better if a man takes a mistress or has an affair instead of being honest?"

I think of my parents. My mother wondering, always wondering, but never having the courage to leave him. Never wanting to. And me, resenting her for her weakness.

"Maybe the rotating muse and the idea of sequential monogamy is a bad analogy..."

Jack rubs the cool of his beer bottle over his forehead and along his neck. There is a bead of perspiration pausing on his Adam's apple, balancing off the slight slope. The muscles are long and taut on either side of his strong neck. His work shirt is open at the collar. There is an indentation where the neck meets the collar bone, as if a thumb had gently pressed to shape that one spot. The bones rise from the indentation, hide themselves behind the veil of his cotton work shirt. But they are there still, running in broad, straight lines all the way to his squared shoulders. Necessity, sweat and toil have created his body as diligently and precisely as any master sculptor could of stone or clay.

"What was I saying?" I ask him, surprised at my wandering mind.

"Something about replacing one love for another." He smiles.

"Yes, well..." Suddenly I feel shy, awkward. Come on, this is Jack! My old pal. "I think I will have that beer after all."

Jack wanders over to the fridge. And with his back to me he can finally ask the question that's been on his mind since he first laid his hands on *The Imaga Dea*.

"So, have you given up on men then?"

"No. Not at all. I love men. But, I guess there are times that attraction just takes over and it transcends gender. I mean, why should we be prisoners of sexual labels? Come on, haven't you ever been attracted to a man before?"

"Hell no. Too hairy and smelly." He hands me a beer. "So what is it about her?"

I shrug. Even I'm not sure why she holds such power over me.

"Her beauty, I suppose. Her smell. Her selfish disdain. When I'm with her I feel more alive, even if she frustrates me most of the time. She laughs at me. Belittles me. But I put up with it because I'd rather have that than nothing. Anyhow, it doesn't really matter because the sculpture is done and she's moved on to someone else."

"Oh fuck," sighs Jack. "You got it bad and that ain't good."

"Oh, please!" I roll my eyes at him. "You sound like a bad country and western song."

"What? You think because I'm a man that I don't know about love?"

Jack jumps off his work bench and hoofs it over to the kiln. He checks the thermometer. Then stands there, for no reason, with his back to me.

"I wrote the fuckin' book on love."

*****

One out of four people suffer from serious depression. Twenty percent will travel the path of self destruction. It is the primary contributor in over sixty percent of suicides. But it is not the day-in and day-out depression that determines when one might jump. It is the sudden impulse, subtly triggered, that pushes one to the brink.

I go into my studio, wanting to work, but am unable. *The Imaga Dea* is in Jack's capable hands, and there is nothing now that inspires me to work. I pick up some clay, press my fingers into it. But the gesture is anaemic, half hearted. What is there to do now, after *The Imaga Dea*? What image could now fill my thoughts, haunt my dreams and drive my fingers to knead, mould, and shape? I have always maintained that the inspired vision must spring from the mind, untainted and pure. Athene bursting from Zeus' head, born not of the physical but of the inspirational. But no visions come to mind. The Perian Well has gone dry and I'm thirsting.

The phone rings in the other room, and because there is no work to consume me I pick up.

"Is that life-sized Narcissist still wasting all your time?"

"Wow. That's the pot calling the kettle black!"

"I'm offended. Come on. You don't really think that?"

It's Boris. I'm not sure why, but I am actually glad to hear his voice. Perhaps because I know that he is one of the few people who understand that when a piece of work is finished there is no rejoicing. Only a sense of letting go. Post partum depression.

"She's being fired."

"Finished then? No more need of your muse?" Boris laughs.

"No," I say, "I have no more need of her now."

"Good, because I met your replacement. She paraded him around the gallery."

"Do you think the attraction is that he's from India," I ask, immediately regretting it.

"No. I think the attraction is that he is a filmmaker. Ours is a dying art. His is on the rise. Oh don't worry, it's just a phase. She'll get bored with him too. She gets bored of everyone."

"Speak for yourself."

"That boredom was very mutual my dear."

"Mutual Boredom. That could be an interesting piece." I imagine two bodies, once taut with desire, now used up, tired and filled with contempt for the very flesh that had inspired passion. I could make it from wax. Build it up, layer by layer. The first layer, attraction, the next layer want, then fulfillment and finally disregard... Wax would be so soothing after clay. Warm and softening for my roughened hands. Eventually the wax would have to be bronzed, but I could skip a step with wax. Go directly into a negative mold and then pour in the heated bronze and just melt the wax away...

"I think I finally have an idea for a new piece. Mutual Boredom." I change the topic from Premika and my replacement.

Boris laughs.

"I am going to do it in wax I think," I continue.

"Did you need me to come over and pose for you? Get naked? I am the perfect choice for a piece called *Boredom*."

Now it's my turn to laugh. Although I am not enjoying myself enough to stay on the phone. Who could imagine that boredom could be a muse?

Free from phone chat, I pull what wax I have out of storage. I light a candle and place a dented pot above it. There's another pot, a larger one, on the stove melting more. As it liquifies, I pour from the larger to the smaller pot. This wax will cool a bit, but it must remain warm enough to be pliable.

The studio fills with the heavy odor of melted wax. I wonder how much of it evaporates into the air? And if I were to spend years working with it, breathing it in, what then? Would my lungs fill with the soft brown material, layer by layer until, like a pair of candle molds, I could put a long wick down my windpipe and into them. Then I could contain a candle flame inside of me. I, too, could be as brilliant as a flame. As bright and burning and all consuming.

I work quickly. Bending some wire, pouring on wax, shaping two figures. I warm a knife to melt through their bodies, separate them a little. I run the heated edge of the blade over her backside to make the surface as smooth as softened skin. Who are these figures really? My mind wanders back to Premika. Suddenly I see her in the wax, in the female nude. Her back, her legs, her breasts.

There is no way around around it. The other figure will have to be Boris.

CHAPTER 7

Most major cities have at least one man-made structure tempting one to leap. San Francisco has the Golden Gate Bridge while further up the coastline Vancouver boasts a glorious last view from the Lion's Gate Bridge. For lovers and poets alike there is The Eiffel Tower in Paris, whereas in London, the whispering gallery encourages a jump from St. Paul's Cathedral, whisking the devout straight to God. Toronto's mythical structure is not the CN Tower, however. Why climb to the heavens in order to spiral back down? In Toronto there are two places to avoid when hopelessly depressed: the Bloor Street Viaduct, a bridge that crosses the Don River, joining the east and west sides, and, of course, the subway system. Underground, and just a little closer to Hades. The Toronto Transit System. Known to the locals as the T.T.C. *"The better way to go."*

There is no 'better way' to get to the Beaches. No direct transport. An eastbound ride to Victoria Park and then a wait for a southbound bus to take me to Kingston Road. I wait with both my hopes and my portfolio tucked under my arm. Why am I here? Jack. It was Jack's crazy idea to approach an antique store instead of a gallery. To sell on commission until I am better known.

Almost an hour of transit and I arrive at *Beaches Art And Treasures*. The awning in front is a throwback to the fifties. The signage has seen better days with its cracked green lettering. Even the windows look tired and defeated. I take a big breath and ready myself. There is an old fashioned bell attached to the door which rings out as I enter. A little man shuffles in from behind a worn dark green velvet curtain. He's gruff looking, with wiry hair, big earlobes and heavy framed glasses that dwarf his round, dimpled face. He sees my portfolio right away and immediately seems perturbed that his door bell rang and disturbed him. All around him is an unorganized mess of junk and antiques.

"One man's trash is another man's treasure," he shrugs as I scan the interiors of his street front shop. "Can I help you find something in particular?"

Then I see it. It's instant love. There really is no other word for it. Every stroke of her brush seems a beat of my heart. I can't help but wonder how this tired little man could possibly have found this unknown treasure. It must have been part of an estate purchase and to score the oil, he had to buy the lot.

"Can hardly pay the rent these days. Nobody's buying art. Nobody's buying good furniture. Everyone's home looks like a hotel room. All shiny and plastic! A travesty! My life is a travesty!"

His words are just a background of sound. White noise. I point to the canvas and interrupt him. "Look at the landscape reflected in the pane of glass. The woman sits inside where it's so clean and sterile while outside there is a dense and lush landscape beckoning. But the woman doesn't look at the landscape, she looks at the reflection instead. Here," I gesture to the glass in the door, "you see the trees outside, but you also see her face, longing to be outside yet caught somehow inside. She daren't go out and so she remains liminal."

"Liminal? Now that's a big word for a little girl."

"Trapped between the reality of the world beyond her and the reflection she sees and knows so well. This is the painting of an outcast. Someone who feels she doesn't belong. Someone from away."

"Ah," says the little man, "you presume a woman painted it because the subject is female."

"No," I say, "Plenty of men have painted female subjects. I am almost certain a woman painted it because I suspect I know who the artist is."

Christiane Pflug. The extraordinary painter who would, at the age of 35, board the ferry to cross Lake Ontario, and travel to Hanlan's Point. The water and the nature would seem at odds with the city-scape diminishing on the horizon. She'd stare at it, her eyes growing more and more heavy with sleep. This is what she wanted. Escape. Far away from her homeland and far away from everything familiar. She would die this way. By her own making.

"Well there's no signature so who knows? Now if you were sure you wanted to buy it, then I would see if I could have it authenticated somehow. But you would have to put a deposit down. It's cheap. I could do seven-fifty..."

I remind him that I came to show him slides of my work. To unload my art, not to acquire more. He shakes his diminutive head and tells me that he has *real* artists that he can't sell. Paintings he acquired through estate clearances, from honest to goodness collectors. So how did I figure he could sell my work? Me, an unknown.

"If this were only America! At least they pay for art there. They know what they like, and they buy it. There's money there. Real money. In New York a lawyer makes three times what he'd make here. So they have to spend it on something. But here? You have to tell them it's good and even then they don't believe you. They try to get a better deal. They talk you down. But in America," he shook a stubby finger in my face, "in America they take risks."

In America, it is estimated that well over a million suicides are attempted by adults every year. They take risks.

"Have you tried the major galleries?" I ask him. "The Art Gallery of Ontario has a Pflug, so does the National Gallery, they might be able to authenticate it."

"Those bastards!?" he snatches up my portfolio and, to his credit, shuts his mouth long enough to flip through the slides of my bronzes and plasters.

I return to my reverie of colour and shape. It is unlike the work I usually love. I usually go for texture and depth. This has neither. There is only a sense of quiet despair. You want to reassure the figure, tell her that it will work out all right. But that would be a lie. There is no escape in reflection. Not in the reflection of a window, nor in the reflection of a lake.

"You're good, but you're not a name. I can't help you." He abruptly closes the portfolio.

"It's okay," I tell him. "Thanks for your time."

*****

My great regret was not that he turned me down but that I later told Premika and Victor about the small, perfectly painted canvas. Victor was his usual, generous self, picking up the bill. I couldn't have afforded the restaurants he frequented and so, although I was relieved whenever he picked up the bill, I was also reminded that I was eating out of my league. Il Posto, Splendidos, Truffles in The Four Seasons. Never could it be the places Premika and I went without him. The Rivoli. The Queen Mother. The Bamboo. And countless greasy spoons.

"Would you mind if I bought it?" he asked as he calculated the tip. Twenty percent. It's always twenty percent unless the service was not to his liking.

"What? The *Pflug?*" I asked, somewhat aghast.

"If it is a *Pflug*. You said it wasn't signed."

"It must be her. You see most artists work a whole canvas. They sketch out the entire painting and then add detail bit by bit. Christiane Pflug worked a tiny bit at a time. Finishing a few square inches entirely before moving on. This piece is unfinished, but what has been painted is completely done. Detailed, painted entirely. That's why it isn't signed, there's a bit in the corner completely bare. Just canvas. She must have been working on it when she killed herself."

Premika looked up suddenly.

"How did she kill herself?" she asked.

"She went to Toronto Island and floated away. Drifted away, drugged I guess."

Victor laughed. It was just too romantic for him. But Premika was alert now, interested.

"Why? Why did she do it if she was such a talented artist?"

"Who knows? I don't think she left a note. I suspect it is because she was an outcast. German, here at a time when Germans weren't liked much. And of course her husband was a task master. A real Svengali," I said, looking directly at Victor.

Victor ignored my sly jab. All he knew was that if Premika was fascinated by the idea of the painting then he should acquire it for her.

"Was it her first attempt?" Premika asked. "Had she threatened to kill herself before?"

"She attempted on numerous occasions. Her daughter said that her suicide was the only thing she actually ever did for herself."

Victor seemed uncomfortable. Perhaps she told him about the threat she made to her father. Perhaps he found the conversation morbid or impolite. Once it was taboo to discuss religion or politics at a dinner table but now those topics are quite common over a meal. It is AIDS and suicide that are now taboo.

"I'll put a down payment on it until he can authenticate it for me," he changed the subject.

"You... you mean buy it for... for yourself?" I stuttered. I couldn't quite grasp the fact that he could consider purchasing something without so much as seeing it.

"Well, yes. It's cheap. It sounds like a smart buy. Why not? Where is this place again?" he asked without a trace of obvious malice.

And I told him! I actually told him. Why? Why, why, why, why, why? That painting was meant for me. It was my soul she painted without even knowing me! It was my soul smeared on the surface of that canvas. Mine. Not his - and not Premika's!

"I wonder why she didn't leave a note?" Premika mused. "You would think that she would want to leave something behind."

"Most people who are serious about killing themselves don't leave notes. It's a myth, the suicide note. A convenient contrivance used in movies."

"Really?" She thought for a minute. "I wonder how I would do it. Nothing too painful."

"I think everyone has an exit in mind. A way of going. I was once at a subway station..."

But before I could tell my story, before I could say that it was the very day I met Premika, Victor interrupted, put an end to it.

"Enough. Suicide is just plain selfish and stupid. There is no good reason for it! The question should not be why she did or didn't sign a suicide letter. The question should be why she didn't sign that painting!" Victor steered the subject to his advantage. "But it does give me the chance to get her unfinished work at a great price!"

The very next day Premika would leave me a message, her voice, happy and triumphant, broadcasting itself into my weary world.

"Just wanted to thank you. The painting's great, we picked it up today. Victor talked the guy down another hundred dollars. He's such a genius. Oh, and guess what? Turns out that if it was that painter you told us about, she studied fashion design in Paris! Just like I was going to! Talk about serendipity. You've got to come and see it."

Serendipity. I hate that word. Almost as much as I hate the overuse of the word *genius*.

*****

From the moment I entered Victor's newly bought condo, I was drawn to the small canvas over the mantle. The painting that should have been mine.

"It's just such a lovely piece. It speaks to me."

"Really? What does it say to you?" Victor laughed. "Look, if it means so much to you, you can trade it for the sculpture you're doing of Premika."

"*The Imaga Dea* would be nice," Premika piped in from the kitchen. Her voice seemed casual, without premeditation.

"Great," said Victor, "take the painting and find somewhere to hang it in your little apartment."

"I'm afraid I don't have any purple in my apartment. It wouldn't match."

I meant to show him how crass I felt he was. I meant to insult him. But Victor wasn't one to be insulted. He found it quite funny.

"Next thing you know, she's gonna get me to throw in my velvet cushions and drapes too. You may as well take the painting tonight. It's coming down anyhow. Got my eye on a Varley."

"You've got more than one wall, Victor."

"I know, but that nude painting of Premika is going over the fireplace. You know the one?"

"The one Boris did?" I ventured.

"Right. Not that it's worth much, but it has sentimental value for Premika."

Premika brought some hors d'oeuvres to the table. The usual fare: salmon pâté, olives and cheese. She placed them beside a basket of toasted bread. She seemed comfortable in his new home. Like she belonged there. I suddenly felt hungry.

"It's not the best painting in the world, but it is the first nude portrait she ever posed for," Victor continued. I glanced at Premika and she shrugged. The painting had no sentimental value for her. Victor needed to own it, and display it, simply because it was of her and he couldn't bear that someone else might possess her image.

"The Varley will go there," he indicated a space of wall between his butter-leather sofa and a small mahogany bookshelf filled with hard cover, first edition books, each signed by the author. "So I don't know where I'd hang the Pflug. Where would you put her?"

"Apart from my apartment?" I quipped.

Victor laughed. God, he was almost charming.

"I would put her somewhere by herself. There is something solitary about her. She shouldn't compete with other work. I'd hang her from your ceiling by two chains, in front of your wall of windows."

"Well it's a moot point because it's yours as soon as we agree on a price for the statue you made."

"She isn't finished yet."

"If she had her way she would never finish it!" Premika piped in.

I steered the conversation away from my sculpture. I ate. Food, plates of it, kept appearing. I wondered if they actually cooked it all, or had it catered and ready in the kitchen. I chewed and I listened to Victor's plans for his future. And when Victor finished detailing how successful his film company would become, how it would span two cultures because he would make English films in an Indian setting, he spoke of the value of marketing and the need to live in the public eye.

"Premika understands this. The power of the public eye."

She understood him only too well. She lived in the public eye. But if that eye should blink, what then?

"She is the perfect actress for both the Hindi and Western market. They would love her in both worlds. The Indians like their female stars to be lighter skinned. And here, well you know only too well, she is exotic. Period pieces with English colonials in India and the beautiful but accessible Indian woman. Beautiful to both cultures."

"I didn't know she could act." I turn my head and address Premika, "When did you decide to become an actress?"

"It's always been something I've wanted to do."

"Since when? Have you even studied acting?"

Victor laughed, "Oh come on, she's a natural. She did a commercial for me in Paris and the camera loves her. Very emotive on screen. Now if she stopped being so lazy and learned some Hindi she could act in both the English and Hindi versions of the films. Two for the price of one! Ah, it's okay, we can re-voice her."

Premika doesn't see that she's a commodity. That the very thing that has made her feel like she doesn't belong in either culture is being used to sell her to both cultures. Or perhaps she does see it. Perhaps this is the first time that she feels she has found her place. Being the inspiration for one work of art, seen by only a few, could hardly compare to the promise of becoming an international star. How could I possibly compete with that? She could be the star in both worlds. And her father would have to acknowledge her.

"You should let Victor market you," she said.

"Oh, I'm not ready for that."

"You just need to be more recognizable. Become a name, create an image for yourself. I'm always amazed at artists. You work in images. You understand images. But for the most part, you fail to create an image for yourself. That is why directors need producers. And also to find them the money!" Victor said.

"I would hope that my work might be salable because of its own merit."

"It doesn't work that way anymore. You can't actually sell a product without selling an idea. Look at Nike. Do you really think that their shoes are so much better? No, they are selling the lifestyle that goes with it. The swoosh says 'just do it,' and that speaks to our generation."

"The swoosh?"

"Every product must have a brand."

"First of all, I don't think of art as 'product.' Secondly, the very nature of art is idea. Every visual work, for me, at least, begins with an idea. Even film begins with an idea, a story!"

Victor drained his glass of red wine. He was very pleased with the vintage, although his expense was somewhat wasted on me. The wine tasted good, but what do I know of rare vintages and labels? Once emptied, he flicked his index finger against the rim of the glass and a rich ring sang out.

"Film is called an art form but it is more of a business. Who is going to invest in a movie in order to lose money?'

"There are auteurs..."

"In Canada, maybe. You have your government agencies to help finance your auteurs but, at the end of the day, you only see your precious Canadian content if you go to the film festival. I know, I had a lovely little film here. About an Irish soldier in India who defects and runs off with a beautiful Indian woman. You could have played that role Premika!"

Premika kisses his cheek before picking up plates. How domestic she seems.

"If businessmen don't invest in art, then how will they be remembered?" I ask him.

"Oh my God, your boyfriend Boris is right! You are old fashioned," he laughed.

I wasn't sure which was more upsetting, that he should think Boris was my boyfriend or that Boris would tell him I'm old fashioned. Out of touch. Redundant. Premika must have told him that Boris was my boyfriend; Boris would never refer to himself that way. I looked at Premika, but she didn't look at me. There were other courses to deliver.

"Most people are too busy to care these days. We no longer have the leisure time to think about art or poetry. It takes a lot of energy and commitment to build an empire."

"Please. Empires have been built and destroyed throughout history, but who remembers the financier? Look, Victor, anybody can name a seventeenth century Dutch painter. Vermeer, Rembrandt... But can you name a seventeenth century Dutch merchant?"

"People remember the Medici family. I mean, I know they weren't Dutch but they were wealthy merchants," Premika piped in and I suddenly realized how quiet, how not-present she had been.

"Of course. They were rich. They were a prominent family. But why are they remembered? Because of the many artists they employed and patroned. Walk through the Uffizi Gallery and most of the work there was paid for by the Medicis. And that is why we remember them."

Victor must have noticed Premika's defeated expression, her subtle pout. He got up, wrapped his arms around her and kissed her. "Great meal. How about some coffee and cognac? And then let's tell her our news."

*****

I can hear Victor whispering to her in the next room. His voice, hushed and intimate. I cannot escape the sounds of their private murmurs; my ear is too keenly resting on the wall.

I should have gone home but I drank too much. First there was a fiery cognac that burned my throat and heated my chest. Then out came an aged bottle of port which Victor carefully decanted so that the sediments could fall to the bottom of the finely cut crystal. My body sank heavily into the sofa. My mind was emptying. I fell deeper and deeper into the cushions as Victor's voice rumbled further and further away like retreating thunder.

Whisper, whisper. Such sotto voce seductions persist beyond the wall that separates us. My surroundings whirl and dance to the timbre of their voices. If I put a foot on the floor, will it make them stop?

I plump the cushion and close my eyes, but their sounds persist. He must be inside her now. His cock pushing a path into her. I could never compete with his divining rod. Never bend to her wetness, her heat. Never feel her sweat or struggle under my weight as I crush her, enter her and fill her with my life force. I would never find my way inside her messy labyrinth. Not physically. I couldn't. But I *have* interpreted her, captured her soul in a moment.

Victor can have her physical body. It will only grow old in time anyhow. But that part of her that is youthful and pure, that part that is more than her body, I have known. I have penetrated her with my art. As deeply and as hard as I could. She went to him no longer a spiritual virgin. And now domesticity is already wearing away her intrinsic being.

God, I must be drunk.

They're still making love in the master bedroom. He thrusts, she inhales sharply, over and over again. A locomotive rhythm. A persistent acceleration. Didn't they drink as much as I?

Their throaty sounds make me yearn for taste and touch. For flesh. Flesh that is young and supple and yearning. Flesh that desires mine. Not a body that comforts and consoles, but the heated flesh of urgency. Urgency that comes of desire. Not love or consolation but the need to possess, if only for a moment. I loved her. I penetrated her. But my desire for her was never consummated. Never returned. I held her in my statue, but I couldn't hold her in my arms. I can't hold anyone. I never could.

The whispering stops. They've finished now. Maybe now we can all get some sleep.

*****

My body is cold. Shaky. I sit up in bed and feel the dampened bed clothes. My head is stuffy, my eyes are sore, my neck aches.

I dreamed of the falls last night. Of water rushing over the edge. There I was, on a tightrope, trying to balance. Head spinning. And the safety of ground miles away, whirling in my focus. One step and I am falling. Through the mist. But, before I hit rock or water, I awoke with a start and a racing heart.

It's a sure sign. Whenever I dream of water I wake with bleeding. Period cramps. And a hangover as well. I try to wipe the small blood stain from their sheets, but succeed only in smearing it across the pale pastel pattern. I panic. I could strip the bed, leave the sheets in a pile somewhere. Or hide them. No, I'll take them home with me. Wash them and return them. But then Victor might think that I stole them.

Why am I so embarrassed? It's only blood. Perfectly natural. I'll strip the bed, leave the sheets in their laundry hamper and then leave. Quietly.

I throw on a flannel shirt to warm myself. Couldn't belong to Premika. Must be his. I pull on my jeans and cram my silk shirt into my purse.

I tiptoe past the dinner debris and pause briefly in front of their bedroom. The lightest touch and the door swings open silently. They are both naked, only the rumple of sheets concealing parts of their bodies. Premika's bare leg dangles off the edge of the bed. Her face is pressed into a pillow. Her shoulders and breasts escape the folds of linen. But across her chest, claiming her, is the draped arm of Victor. He stirs slightly. I pull the door shut. Gather my things and escape into the harsh glare of morning light.

CHAPTER 8

I descend down, down, down into the Underworld. Where is the pomegranate now with its binding seeds of knowledge and retribution? Persephone had to be dragged below, but I descend freely.

8:15. A train thunders overhead. Wind echoes through the tunnels. A silver train brakes to a stop. Doors open, whistles blow. No, I will wait here. Face the open tunneled mouth and listen. But then, that voice inside me, that other woman, whispers to me. Dares me. *Step closer, step closer.* I inch a bit closer. Feel the breeze from the tunnel. *There now. Just another inch.*

Sacrifice. It is the currency of love. Through it we prove our intention, display our devotion and show ourselves to be worthy. Love matures through each sacrifice. It yields its youthful caprice and moves beyond its nascent flirtation. But what sacrifice have I ever made, could ever make, for anyone I love?

I step back. The yellow line is at least six inches from me now. How could I play such a foolish game after the sacrifice my mother made for me? My mother sacrificed her very identity for my father and me. She sacrificed her dreams, her freedoms and her comfort. And I loved her in return, but with the selfishness of a child, wanting her approval, wanting to always be the apple of her eye, knowing that I would never be able to be as selfless as she. My ego, and my talent, would never allow it.

I did offer to delay art college. I did! I offered to stay at home, be with my mother. But she said, "*No. I'm guilty of wasting my own life, I won't waste yours as well.*" As I filled my head with art, she filled her veins with morphine, easing her pain and erasing the memories that brought her sorrow. But her whole life was comprised of pain and when she killed it, there was nothing left. By the time she was admitted to the hospital, she hardly knew who I was. I was all but forgotten.

My train arrives. A red one. I leave the tunnel, the wind and the temptation to jump behind me. I get on. The doors close and I am safe. Safe from lovers and voices. Safe from temptation. And safe from the guilt of my selfish being.

*****

8:45. I make tea and wander about feeling, what? Lost in my own home.

Did the father of classical sculpture ever feel this way? Did Phidias wander about his studio, aimlessly fueled by discontent and dread? Surely not. Not back then; neurosis is a modern ailment. Bi-polar, borderline, manic-depressive are all modern words for what? Melancholia. Yup, that's what I suffer from. Especially in the blue hours of morning. Phidias would have had no time for inward reflection. No time to skulk about with down-turned lips. No, he was too busy sculpting the images of gods, greedy gods, wanting more than immortality.

Funny that the sculptor is immortalized but not his work. Oh there are many reproductions. From the earliest Romans to modern souvenir hawkers, Phidias's work has been knocked off century after century, repeated and remembered through watered down clones. There is only one original object of his making. A small cup. A cup with an inscription written in formal, not the usual familial, inscription. The cup, therefore, must have been made for something greater than the public. The cup was a token of affection, made for a god.

Why can't I keep the company of gods? It isn't fair. I have neither the faith of the Catholic nor the madness of the

Pagan. My soul is lacking. That's what is wrong with me. I have an immature soul. I meet so many people who tell me that they are old souls. They brag about the age of their invisible selves. But not me! I have no faith, no reassurance of an afterlife. *Be in the world but not of it?* You have to be kidding! I am made of flesh, fueled by breath, and nurtured by sensation. My feet long to take root, to anchor myself in this earth! To belong here.

I blame my father for my undeveloped soul. He maintained that faith was for the weak of mind. I needed to prove my intelligence to be worthy. And so I developed my mind and ignored my soul. All the while, my mother secretly hoping I would choose faith and baptism when I was old enough to decide for myself. In the end I failed them both. My father, by choosing art; my mother, by denying God. I had to. I make idols out of clay. I worship graven images. I have dedicated my life to breaking the second commandment.

I take my mug of tea with me into the studio. Yes, I am attached to *things*. To the corporeal. I want to create. To challenge my mother's invisible god. I do not want to leave this world but to leave *something* in this world. Something of beauty and worth. My art is my only comfort. It is a constant.

Unlike art, love does nothing to extend your memory here on earth. When my mother finally died my father remarried and replaced her. Easy as that! He couldn't stop living simply because she had. He was a practical man, an economist both by nature and trade. And so he found a new love. He got on with it.

Not me. I pledged to lock my heart against love. I strove to be adored instead, choosing greatness over heart's ease. But if I don't ever achieve greatness, then what? If I continue to choose art over love, if I never win my heart's desire, then what meaning will my life hold? People could walk by a crumbling piece of sculpture without a moment's thought. They won't consider the hands that struggled to give it life, the heart that rendered its beauty. If I continue to live my life this way then my existence will have no resonance beyond the breathing of my lungs. If the words "to sculpt" mean "to preserve life," then why does my life seem so meaningless?

Last night Premika announced that she and Victor were going to get married.

*****

"A *Pflug*? You have to be joking!" Boris leans his chair back so that it balances on two legs. "That's no *Pflug*. I don't know where he got such a foolish idea."

How could I have been wrong? The unfinished corner. The choice of colour. The solitary figure reflected in a window that leads to the world beyond her.

"How do you know it's not authentic? There's no signature. It's not complete. It might be one of hers. Maybe she was painting it around the time of her suicide..."

"It isn't a *Pflug*, trust me. I know the painter. I was so surprised to see one of my students' paintings hanging in his condo as though it were a masterpiece. Quite a cosmic joke," he laughs. The chair totters and he regains his balance. "That student was quite proficient, mind you. Could copy any style. But she had no voice of her own, no imagination. You know what she's doing now?"

"What?' I ask.

"Painting murals on the sides of buildings!" He's really laughing now. "It's perfect. Too perfect. Did you tell him it was a *Pflug*? How very clever and cruel of you."

I can't tell Boris that I really did believe the painting to be authentic. Better he think me cruel than stupid.

"Why don't you like him?" I ask.

"What's to like? He's a social climbing parvenue. He isn't making his films to bring insight into another culture, he is making his films to make money! As for the art he collects, he supports wealthy art dealers. Not artists." He shrugs. "I should like him I suppose. Keeps people like me in business."

Victor was going to give me the painting as a deposit on *The Imaga Dea*. If Boris told him the painting was a fake then he tried to pawn it off on me because he knew it was a worthless investment. That son-of-a-bitch! Boris is right about Victor. What's to like?

"He only likes dead artists. Live artists don't have the same social cachet."

Boris rights his chair and sits firmly in his squared seat. His desk and chair are placed strategically in his gallery. The art work behind him serves as a backdrop to his presence. Gold and green billow above his head, pillars of red frame him. He places both elbows on his desk, leans heavily across the scratched but polished oak. Every gesture of his body asks why I'm suddenly visiting him. He cocks his head in anticipation, smiles wryly but doesn't actually ask the question.

"But he *did* buy one of your paintings and you're not dead yet."

"She bought it," he corrects me. Always the teacher.

"With his money and for his apartment."

"Vanity. That's why she bought it. She's losing her bloom already. Victor has possessed her just in time. But you and I, we had her at full blossom, before the petals began to wilt."

"That's very poetic and rather cliché."

"Clichés become so because they are true. Women are like flowers. They bloom at different times. I suppose you want to know what stage you are at?"

"Not really."

"You are still a tight bud. Your petals are screaming to be loosened, but you aren't ready yet."

I shrug him off and roam over to the far wall of the gallery to scan some of his chosen artists' works. A hammered tin relief of a ravaged torso is set between two other reliefs. His body, lean and starved, has a homoerotic draw. It is the detail of the space between the hipbone and tight stomach muscle. That masculine dip that invites you to reach down toward the groin. Clever how the artist stops there, leaving you wanting. On one side of the torso stands another relief, slightly smaller. Three sorrow filled faces staring upward like the three Marys at the base of the cross. But the faces are distinctively masculine. Beautiful, soft and male. The other framing relief is a tin dartboard; a hypodermic needle drilled into the bull's-eye.

A pang of jealousy. The card beneath the work bears Peter's name. My nemesis from art school. He won the scholarship that should have been mine. He takes up space at this gallery. He is, as ever, politically on target.

"What do you think?" Boris gets up from his desk and saunters over to me. He stands so close that I can hear his breath, almost feel it on the top of my head. Every exhalation seems patronizing. It's probably imagined, after all, I know why I came here today and it would be only too easy to sabotage myself.

"Peter's work has improved. Though I could do without the dartboard."

"The dartboard is the point to it all. You like two thirds of the triptych because it is pleasing to the eye. But the dartboard is the truth of the work. Face it, you don't have the heart for the truth."

My critical eye can be quite cold. To praise his work in his demise would be hypocritical.

"He's HIV positive. So what? If a healthy man created that, would it be great? No. You find meaning in it only because you know the artist. And you accuse me of being sentimental!"

"AIDS is a hot topic these days."

"Then you're a faddist."

"Worse. I am a pimp, my dear. My customers are sentimental and I must make a living. You know I am no longer teaching at all now. They've made me redundant. Imagine that?"

"Didn't have anything to do with harassing the female students, did it?" I ask teasingly.

"For fuck's sake. It's art school, not typing class!" He pinches the skin of my forearm between his fingers. "It's in the flesh. The flesh. We're not turning out workers. We are turning out artists! Fucking bourgeois attitudes."

"You used to call me bourgeois, but *I* fucked you."

"Yes, but you were only bribing me."

"Does it matter why I fucked you? Bribery or not, you still got laid."

Boris releases my pinched skin. A red mark raises up from the white flesh.

"I was joking, Boris! Come on. It's not my fault you don't have a sense of humour anymore."

Boris shakes his head slightly. I know him well enough to recognize this is his way of apology. To expect words is to expect too much. But a weary sigh, a shake of the head, the slightest, almost imperceptible shrug is sometimes granted.

"Ah Alexandra. Why did you come here? What do you want?"

"I want a show. I need to show my work. Now I know that you don't want it in your gallery, but I thought perhaps you would know someone who might look at my work."

"Why would I recommend you to someone else?"

"Because, although I don't fit your mandate, you do recognize my proficiency. And also, I'm asking you as a friend."

Boris raises his eyebrow. "As a friend? No. You must ask me as an artist."

I walk away from him. Admire the torso. It's a shame that Peter is dying just as he's beginning to become accomplished. The torso is good. It doesn't need the dartboard as its backup. It doesn't need to be part of an installation. The torso speaks for itself.

"These installations you're so fond of, where will they be in two, three hundred years time? Even if one does make a statement, it is so short lived. The political climate changes, cures are found, society shifts its focus and the work is obsolete. Is anyone going to remember Peter's dartboard when the cure to AIDS is discovered? No. Will they remember Judy Chicago's installation? A bunch of dinner plates that look like women's cunts! Come on!"

"You didn't like the cunts? I'm surprised!"

"Well, I kind of liked them. They were fun, but who's going to compare that to Rodin's Gates Of Hell? "

"Well you could say that about all modern art."

"People will remember Lucian Freud. That's who will be remembered. Not for his politics but for his flesh. You said that art is in the flesh. Remember? Well that's what Freud paints. And that's what I sculpt."

"You think you're comparable to Freud?"

"He's a painter. I'm a sculptor." I shrug off the question.

"Answer me!"

I centre myself, lower my jaw, stare him down. "Yes," I say, "I know I am."

Boris goes to his desk, opens his day timer. "Eight weeks too soon?"

I'm stunned. Heart pounding. A rabbit in the headlights of his offer.

"You don't think that someone comparable to Freud is going to slip through my fingers, do you? Not when I had a hand in making you the artist you claim to be."

"Eight weeks?" I ask.

Eight weeks. I'd have to go through what is in storage at Jack's warehouse, choose the best pieces, rework some, cast others. Eight weeks was far too soon.

"Eight weeks is fine," I agree.

"I will want to see all your work first, you understand. Not that I don't trust your high opinion of yourself."

*****

Eight weeks. I would have to take inventory. Pull pieces out of storage. Maybe even create a new piece. Something small and perfect. Something that will compliment but not compete with *The Imaga Dea*. And I could make a series of plasters from the many maquettes of her. White, opaque willies leading up to her. Each one an incomplete study and then, there she will be, under a light perhaps, basking in the glory of herself. But she has to be finished, sanded. Detailed. There was much work to do.

I walk. Each step a detail of how the show will be revealed. My feet hit the pavement as I pass the angel that rises up on University Street, the relief of Edith Cavell set into the Toronto General Hospital wall, the Henry Moores falling onto the sidewalk in front of the Art Gallery of Ontario. One day, I think, one day, I might be here too. Inside though. Inside these walls. Keeping company with Francis Loring and Florence Wylie.

The street is filled with couples tonight. Late diners and movie goers. Premika's apartment is in the centre of it all, smack downtown at Bay and Bloor. It's unlikely she's there on a Friday. Out on the town, meeting Victor's friends. Seeing and being seen. Still, I decide to ask the concierge to ring up to her. I want to gain entry. Into her apartment. Into her life.

Her apartment is sparse on the best of days. She has a minimalist, almost Japanese, approach to decor. But today it seems barer. Picked clean. Wanting.

"Do you want anything?" she asks.

"No. My apartment is cramped as it is."

"You should take over this place. More room. More comfortable. Then I wouldn't have to clear the furniture out."

I couldn't imagine living amongst Premika's things. Sleeping in her bed while she shared Victor's. And although her apartment is neutral, empty of any relics that might give a clue to her personality or her past, I would feel her over my shoulder just by knowing that she was once there.

Premika starts to laugh. She kicks off her ostrich-skin cowboy boots and falls into the goose down duvet on her queen sized bed.

"God I hate moving."

"Don't then."

"There's no point in paying the extra rent while we wait for the wedding. I'm always at his place anyhow."

"Keep it as insurance."

Premika looks at me blankly. I stare down at her sprawled body. The feathers rising to embrace her. If she were to float up, levitate to the ceiling, the imprint of her body would remain there until the compressed down slowly exhaled to erase her memory.

"It may not work out," I suggest. A weak shrug to casually underline the point.

"You're so pessimistic," she says. "Not a very attractive quality."

"Most marriages don't last, what makes you think that you'll beat the odds? Not a very realistic outlook."

"Did you come over just to be mean? What's with you?"

"Nothing," I say, because that is the expected response.

"Nothing?"

I look at her. Her body is relaxed. It does not reflect the tension in the air. I want to have that body in my arms now, hold it. I do not want to help move her into Victor's condo. Into his world. Into his clutches.

"What's the matter with you? What do you want, Alex?"

I want you to choose me instead. If only I could say it. My face warms with blood. I want to cry for not being brave, for not being able to lay my feelings out before her. I lie down beside her, press my body into her pillows, her bedding, her smell. She rolls onto her stomach so that we are face to face.

"I envy you."

I don't want you to envy me. I just want you to love me.

"You know why I envy you? You have purpose. You know what you want with your life. You don't have to fear a life alone. Of aging. Of being forgotten."

Is that it then? Destined for a solitary life because my desire to create holds the potential for love at bay? Male artists manage somehow. Is it different for us, are we such strange creatures? Do men have different privileges just because their biology is different from ours? Beyond the obvious, the essential difference lies within the seed of our beings. They say that there is a little seed of suicide in all of us, yet men commit suicide three times as often as women. It's not that we are happier or more content; we do attempt suicide four times as often as men. It's just that, once again, men are more successful.

She reaches for my hand. Her cool fingers wrap around mine.

"They're so rough. Like having a man's hand touching you," she says as she runs her smooth index finger over the back of my hand and shakes her head. Then she lifts my palm to her mouth, brushes her tinted full lips over the calloused surface. "Poor baby, you could really do with a manicure. I'll treat you."

"I'll put some cream on them when I go home."

"You work too hard. How long can you go on cutting headstones?" She pauses for a moment before laying our her cards. "You know, Victor was thinking of an image, like the one on the front of the Rolls Royce."

"Mercedes."

"No. A Rolls. I'm sure it's the Rolls Royce."

"The model's name was Mercedes. She was the daughter of the Mercedes car manufacturer but she married the Rolls Royce guy."

"Really? That must have caused some family tensions." Premika stretches her legs. Her jeans are a faded second skin on her thighs.

"What about using *The Imaga Dea* for the production company's logo?" she asks.

"Pardon?" I could not have heard that right.

"How about my image at the start of his films. With his production company name written below?"

"That's just about the dumbest thing I've ever heard."

"It would be a bit like that woman at the start of the MGM pictures. Or is it Columbia? Whatever."

"The Columbia icon. It's supposed to represent America."

"She looks a little like Claudette Colbert."

Suddenly it all made perfect sense. Premika saw herself as a glamorous icon, like those 1930's and 1940's stars. Almost gods and goddesses those early actors were. Bigger than life. Rich when the world was poor, happy when the world was grieving. Shielded from circumstance. An icon fit for human consumption.

"If you sold him the rights to *The Imaga Dea*, you'd never have to worry about money again."

"You have to be joking."

"What are you going to do? Wait around till Boris gives you a show? That's not going to happen and we both know it. You made a bet and lost your chance."

"Actually, I have a show in eight weeks," I tell her. My voice flat and matter of fact. This is not how I imagined telling her. I thought of victory, a glass of champagne perhaps. Celebration.

"So what? It's a one off. You'll be no further ahead than you are now. Your work could be seen world wide. *The Imaga Dea* could be mass produced in India. Sold to tourists the way the *David* is sold is Florence. You'd be famous, rich and successful."

"Maybe they could sell little statues of you alongside Ganesh, Kali and Shiva..." I was on to her. It wasn't about *The Imaga Dea* or my success. It wasn't even about Victor. If she could be in shop windows, at the start of movies and maybe even be a small silverscreen icon herself, then she would have a visual presence all over India and, possibly, the rest of the world. Her father would have to see her, witness her beauty and maybe, just maybe, acknowledge her existence. And she could achieve immortality without the work or sacrifice.

"You're impossible. Victor's right. You are too short sighted to make a success of yourself."

Short sighted is a horrible thing to call an artist because every artist likes to believe she is a visionary. But there is one thing you can call an artist that is worse than saying she is short sighted. One thing only. A sellout.

"You want me to be a *sellout?* Because if I was tempted to sell out, it wouldn't be to Victor. No offense meant."

"Alex, if you want me in your life, you'll have to accept him. We're engaged. I'm in for the long haul."

"But I gave up Max for you," I stammer, knowing the foolishness of the words even as they left my mouth.

"I didn't ask you to!" She rolls onto her back. Looks to the ceiling. I sit up.

"Take your things with you Premika. You'll lose yourself in him. He's that sort of man."

"Are you kidding? He has so much stuff, there's no room for it all. Besides I'm not attached to anything."

"I know," I say, lifting myself from her bed. I fluff my imprint away. Remove any trace of myself.

*****

I exit at Queen Street and walk west toward the Bamboo. He may not be playing. I will just enjoy a solitary drink before taking myself home. I make my way to the familiar entranceway. I leave the concrete and shops of Toronto and enter a world that is Thai and Caribbean, A world of coconut and spice and live music. How many times have I come here before, with Max or Premika?

There are no tables. The room is filled with carefree people. How simple their lives appear. They work their eight hours and then, with wages in hand, they set out to enjoy the remains of their days. No worries of accomplishment. No fear of being forgotten. No desire for immortality.

I sit at the bar, sipping a vodka tonic and stare down at a plate of coconut shrimp with mango chutney. I'm peckish, having missed both lunch and dinner, yet somehow I cannot eat. My desire to celebrate is tainted with loneliness. My sense of adventure feels contrived. My presence is too premeditated.

The second set starts; the patrons clap between mouthfuls. I do not look at the stage. I sip. I bite. I know he's there, trumpet lifted to his mouth. Wetting his lips, darting his tongue into the mouthpiece, around its cold metal rim. I know, only too well, how he readies his instrument before he gets down to playing it. The rest of the band starts. Then his horn wails and blasts across the room. I take the lemon from my glass, bite until citrus tartness is all I taste. Then casually, so casually, turn on my barstool and face the stage.

The saxophonist steps forward, begins a solo. Max moves back, out of focus, drops his trumpet from his lips and begins to survey the room. I hold my breath, not sure if I want to be seen. How to blend, become a chameleon in this rabidly trendy crowd?

He jumps from the edge of the stage, steps between dancers, parting the sea of bodies, cutting a path towards the bar. I shut my eyes, let my body move gently to the music, swaying on my stool.

A hand touches the curve between my neck and shoulders before moving up my nape. Fingers touching the tangles of my hair.

"Hello stranger," I say, slowly opening my eyes, caught in the surreal dream of my own making.

143

He gestures for me to join him on the dance floor. The band members watch with amused interest. Carry on without him. They all know me, the graveyard worker.

I move in his arms. This is all too familiar. We are retracing the steps that had tripped us up once before.

"Max?"

"Shh," he puts his finger to my lips, "the only thing I want to hear is, 'come home with me tonight.'"

"A bit presumptuous," I laugh.

"No," he breathes into my ear, "not presumptuous, hopeful."

"Come home with me tonight," I say, no longer sure which of us is leading.

*****

He works his way down my shirt, from neckline to hem. As each button gives way, he presses his mouth on the revealed flesh. Slowly he works his way down, down, down, exposing me two inches at a time. His lips are swollen from his playing. Tender and raw. But he presses on until I am entirely undone, as is my shirt.

"Go on," he commands as he steps away from me.

I stand in front of him, unsure of what he wants. He goes to my bed, rests his head back on the pillows. *The Barberini Faun* has returned, only this faun is not in my control. This faun is giving the orders. I feel as nervous and objectified as one of my models. He has turned the tables on me. My knees tremble, but he doesn't notice. His focus is elsewhere.

"Panties, please," he indicates with a nod. When did he become so confident? So assertive? What shift has occurred in his life?

"I asked you to take your panties down."

I slip my fingers between the cotton of my panties and the heat of my anxious flesh. The material slides over my hips. He gestures for me to continue. I slide the dampened panties past my thighs and calves and I step out of them. I am vulnerable before him. I stand waiting, expecting that he will strip off and join me in my nakedness. But no.

"Touch yourself."

"Max," I reach my hand out to him. An invitation to join me, meet me half way. Masturbation is too solitary, too sacred to share. Besides, I didn't bring him home so that I could satisfy myself.

"Go on," he urges, "show me how you make love to yourself."

How did Schiele's models feel? Those bony, depraved girls, sprawled and open before him, in postures of self satisfaction. This is how a great model feels. More than on display.

My fingers move into the wetness of my body, obedient to his direction.

The model serves her most intimate self to the artist, offers up her greatest vulnerabilities and asks that the artist, the voyeur, be gentle with his exploitation. She does this for the illusion of immortality, while I offer up this solitary act for the illusion of love.

Max lifts himself from the bed and drops to his knees before me. He gently moves my hands away and buries his face in my dampness.

"I need you to be inside me," I whisper. I want to be penetrated, to be entirely filled, so that loneliness cannot reside within me tonight.

Max leaves me standing, legs slightly parted. His arms are wrapped around my thighs. His fingers grip me, pressing firmly into my flesh, like Hades' grasp on Persephone. His overworked lips wrap around the small rise of my swollen clitoris. I can barely stand.

"Please Max. Please fuck me."

He shakes his head and keeps burying into me. Drinks me until I am drained and weak with want.

"Please," I beg.

But he doesn't stop. I grab onto his hair, my fingers gripping strands between them.

"Oh God!" escapes me and he increases his intent, hurries his tongue until my body is no longer controlled by me but by his touch. Wet runs down the insides of my shaky thighs. His hands rise up, tracing the dampness, to force my legs further apart. I struggle for balance as he pulls open my lips and presses his face harder into me. I can feel the bristle of a day's growth scratching the delicate inner pink flesh.

He slips his fingers inside me. I lose what little control I might have had in reserve. My body collapses on him in a quaking heap. I lie, almost lifeless on the floor. Max rises above me, his face is soaked with the pleasure he has given me. He looks down at me.

"My turn," he says, stooping over to lift me from the floor before carrying me to my bed.

"That was," I start, but he puts his lips to my mouth and swallows my words. His body rolls over mine and, at last, he penetrates my loneliness. All my sorrows are obliterated. For now.

*****

Water runs in the bathroom. Max is washing his face. I should go to him, but my limbs are spent and I have not yet regained control over them. I close my eyes and wait for him to return. When I open them again, he stands, fully dressed above me.

"Are you going?" I ask.

He shifts awkwardly and nods.

"You don't have to."

"Oh you know," he says, mimicking, "sleeping is far too intimate."

I rise up onto my elbows. The sheet slips away long enough to expose the pale pink of a nipple. After making love to this man I am suddenly so self-conscious that this slight exposure seems overwhelming. Something is amiss. I pull the sheet back over me, secure it with a pillow.

"Is someone waiting for you?" I ask.

Max looks away from me. The fact that he doesn't answer, answers my question. Of course there is someone. And does it really matter so much, beyond the sour taste of being replaced? Am I surprised? No.

"Do you love her?"

Max shrugs. "Maybe. I don't know. Too soon to tell."

"Why did you come here tonight?" I ask. But I know the answer. Lovers are like murderers. It's only a question of time before we all return to the scene of the crime.

He touches my cheek with nostalgic affection. "I missed you. I missed making love to you. I thought it would be nice. For both of us. You know me, I live in the moment."

I nod. I feel that seed of darkness taking root deep in the pit of my being. Max goes to the door, but I am already looking through my darkened window, traveling away from him as fast as I can. Escaping beyond the glass.

"Can I see you again?" he asks.

"No. You live in the moment Max. And the moment has passed."

I see my reflection in the darkness of the pane. Behind me is Max. He waits.

"It's easier with her, you know?"

And because I don't turn to face him, he turns away and leaves. My reflection is alone. My face in the glass looks peaceful and composed. It doesn't reveal what I feel inside. I study my features with curiosity. Turn my chin downward and my whole countenance changes from benign to sinister. Focus just beyond the reflection and the image distorts until I am unrecognizable. A subtle blur of unidentifiable traits. No different, no more special than anyone else.

*****

I pour myself a bath. Strip off my clothes and look at my naked reflection in the mirror. My breasts are small, my skin is freckled, my limbs are prematurely sinewy. In my early teens my mother called me gamine. Gamine no longer seems desirable. I look for my most attractive features but my eye keeps being drawn back to my hands. Are they really like a man's? Premika said they felt rough and manly, but how do they look to the eye? The nails are short and, although there is a constant assault of clay and dust upon them, I try to keep them clean. I file them into shape. There are half moons above my cuticles. My fingers are strong. Stronger, perhaps, than most women's, but they aren't overly fleshy or muscular looking. The skin isn't as smooth as Premika's, but I work with my hands. Sculpting takes its toll. In time, no doubt, I will develop arthritis from the constant kneading of clay and from gripping my sculptor's tools. It is a casualty of the trade.

I place my foot into the water, test the temperature with my toe. Too hot. My feet have the sensitivity my hands have lost. They, at least, are the feet of a woman. Narrow, with high insteps. Sensitive to temperature. Ticklish.

I place my foot onto the hot water of a poured bath. Hold it to the scalding heat until it adjusts to the temperature, then slowly lower it until the foot touches the bottom of my claw foot tub. This is my great luxury item. Although Premika has complained about my cramped quarters, my makeshift studio and my outdated, undecorated apartment, this top floor offers other benefits. Morning light above the trees, no footsteps overhead and a wonderful old bathtub.

I stand with both feet in and let the steam wrap around my body before I lower myself down. I prepare to wash away the disappointment of the day. To hush that voice in me that cries out, "Choose me! Choose me! Love me!"

The flesh below the water surface is turning pink. A vibrant pink that only the fairest skin turns. A bit too much sun, hot water, an embarrassing moment, and we are betrayed by our epidermis. From bisque to lobster in a nanosecond. But the heat works its wonders. It penetrates my skin, makes its way to my muscles and eases the knots contained there. Premika is right about one thing. My day job is taking its toll on my body. I feel it deeply under the skin. But my flesh remains unmarked. I am unmarked and unremarkable.

Michelangelo *was* marked. Marked by the hand. A peer, a fellow sculptor, approached him, saying, "*They say you are a genius, but you will wear the mark of my fist forever.*" He broke Michelangelo's nose, left the mark of his jealous hand on the face of a genius.

I ease my head back, wet my hair so that it floats around my face in the water. I feel myself relaxing in this warm womb. I could fall asleep here, but that's always a mistake. The water turns cold, you wake with a shock and all that effort to relax is undone.

If only I could create something that inspired that level of passion, something that would compel a stranger to hit me in the face out of jealousy. Then it wouldn't matter that I'm second choice in love. It wouldn't matter that someone is always put ahead of me. Victor. My father's mistress. Max's new girlfriend. Premika even. Didn't Boris choose her while he was still with me?

I drain the tub, wrap myself in a towel and catch a clouded glimpse of the rosy tone my skin has taken on. Perhaps I could be painted. There is a distinct colour to my flesh. But I could never be sculpted. My body could never inspire anything like *The Imaga Dea*. Let alone anything as perfect as *The David* or *The Barbarini Faun*. But why make such comparisons? *The Imaga Dea* isn't made of marble any more than I am made of clay.

CHAPTER 9

On weekends the trains are less crowded. There is no rush hour horde, pushing and elbowing, jostling for space. Fighting for a place to get to work or home from work. Imagine that in Tokyo men with white gloves and sticks fill the subway cars. Cram commuters in until filled to capacity, then bar the rest from boarding. Packed away like sardines in a can. But without the brine.

The Imaga Dea is fired and Jack has reassembled her parts. She is with him now, waiting for me. I am nervous. More nervous than I have ever been on a date or before an exam. More nervous than I was the first time I flew or drove a car. More nervous than I was when Premika first peeled off her clothes for me.

I grip the subway seat. There is gum underneath. Tacky and pliable. Somewhat fresh. A student from my class sculpted in gum. Sticky little figures of grey. When asked what was the hardest part about working in his chosen material, he answered that his jaw was still sore from all the chewing! Now I wonder why he just didn't harvest from under tables and chairs. It would have been a service to diner patrons and subway riders across the city. And surely the press would have helped him to be better known.

I could be better known. I could sell the rights of *The Imaga Dea* to Victor and make enough to quit my day job. I could sculpt full time. Do interviews and talk about art in journals and magazines. So why won't I do it? Because, I suppose, I know that if Victor can give her greater fame than I, then I will lose her forever. If I hand him *The Imaga Dea* then he will have all the power and I will be left with nothing. No, *The*

Imaga Dea has to win public approval without the aid of Victor. She must win on her own merit.

****

Jack goes over the areas that need work. The holes, punctured for the escape of her heated exhalation, must be filled, sanded and finished. Every noticeable seam or joining mark must disappear so that she looks as though she were born fully formed, complete.

"You smell good."

"I washed."

"Got a date?" Jack inquires.

"No."

"You didn't gussy yourself up for me, did you?"

"No."

"Didn't think so."

Jack picks up a small corner of sandpaper. It's a fine grain, very gentle. He rubs it along her collar bone until a powdery film rises to the surface. He leans forward and blows on her neck. The clay debris rises from her body in a talcum cloud.

"So? What do you think?" I ask him.

"What do I think? I think you better have me help you do the finishing. You don't want to fuck this one up."

I throw my arms around him in an embrace. I feel Jack's body stiffen a little. And so I step back. Punch his arm. Remind him that we're friends.

"Now you just have to do it again in marble. Better get on that. Eight weeks isn't very long and the marble awaits you! It would be nice for your show."

"Why are you on about marble all the time? It's rather elitist for someone so..."

"So what? Working class?" Jack's tone is oddly ironic.

"It's just that marble isn't everyone's best medium," I back-pedal.

"I don't agree. Name one, just one, of the great sculptors who isn't known for his marbles."

I laugh. I imagine Rodin and Michelangelo, each with a pouch full of alleys, crouching down to a competitive game of marbles. Rodin's tiger eye hits Michelangelo's agate and suddenly he is out of the game. Replaced by the younger sculptor.

"Easy," I say, and Jack thinks I'm laughing because I have the answer. "Donatello. All his marbles together don't compare to his *Repentant Mary*."

Standing at about 188 centimetres tall, a ravished, time worn, Mary Magdalene looks beautiful in her aged decay. Traces of past beauty are subdued by the suffering of her chosen path. Abstinence and fasting have taken their toll. She is crooked, drawn -- a wise crone now. She wears rags. Her wooden flesh hangs off the bone. A hag. Yet one of the most beautiful, most inspiring pieces I have ever seen. Donatello worked in marble as well. He too created a marble statue of *David*, but it didn't compare to Michelangelo's. As Michelangelo would carve the ultimate *David*, so Donatello would sculpt the ultimate *Mary Magdalene*. In wood.

"I thought you didn't care for pity in a work," Jack challenges. Most unlike Jack. But then, he has been working extra hours. Making up for time I am missing while I prepare for the show. I can tell by the dust on his jeans and the dirt on his work shirt that he must have gone in this morning. Done a few hours on a Saturday then hurried home to meet me here. He clearly hasn't yet showered. The stone dust must be irritating him. Getting under his skin.

"No," I start cautiously, "I said that tenderness and greatness don't go hand in hand. The *Repentant Mary* isn't tender. Quite the opposite, she has survived the test of time. Her bent body represents an incredible will. An inner strength. She has embraced suffering and wears it in every feature and nuance."

"Embracing suffering is just too romantic for me. Sorry."

"Did I do something to upset you? You know I appreciate everything you've done for me." I gesture toward *The Imaga Dea*. "And her."

"It's just," Jack hesitates, shifts his weight from foot to foot. "I just find it all a bit disturbing. I mean, she's remarkable and all. Beautiful even. But I couldn't live with that piece. Honestly, I can't wait to be rid of her. I think you should store her away till you're ready to show her."

"I didn't realize that she had that much power over you."

"It's not the power she has over me. Look, I can see it's a work of art but I also see that it is still just a pile of clay. Shaped and fired, but clay all the same. No, what is disturbing to *me* is the power she has over *you*."

Power over me? I may admire her, love her even, but how can my own creation have power over me? I gave it life. I have power over her.

"There's a little work to do on her. Can we get her to my studio?"

"Do the work here. Why move her twice. Eight weeks isn't long. I could live with her if I knew it was temporary. Don't get me wrong. It is a great work. Just a bit difficult for me."

Was it my piece or my relationship to the piece he was having trouble with? Or was it my relationship to the model who inspired it? Or did he think that my work was beyond him? That I had continued to grow since our college days while he had figured out a way to enjoy his work, without committing to it fully. He had found a balance I would never know and, in doing so, would always need Amadeo and his place of work.

"Can I take you for dinner? Just to thank you for everything?"

"Tempting, but I've made other plans. Hey, if I knew you washed up so well, I would'a turned down the other offer."

I look at Jack quizzically. He shifts his weight and laughs, trying to brush it off. I give him the silent standoff until he fesses up.

"Amadeo asked me to escort his daughter to some company dance, or something. Her fiancé dumped her and she already had the tickets. Anyhow, he said she was upset and wasn't going to go and that she really should. So there you have it."

"Be careful," I warn. "I think old Amadeo might have plans for you."

"Hah. It's a mercy date. That's all. Let me open the storage room for you, then I really have to shower."

Jack goes next door to his storage unit, although in actuality it stores more of my work than his. I turn my attention to the piece dominating his loft space. The colour of this fired clay is almost a flesh hue. A bit more amber, more tanned. Premika is a slightly paler version. Two shades lighter than this earthy replica. Step back a few paces though, and one might believe it to be skin. The clay is porous. There are some fine lines, some texture to the form. I must use a very gentle hand when I sand her.

But will she answer Boris's mandate? Boris believes that creating an image of the human body without assigning it a political stance is outdated and pretentious. But the human soul has always needed to create the figurative in three dimensions, whether it be those early fertility idols, the bare breasted European figureheads or the lonely *inuksuk* that rises up in the barest, northern tundra. What drives the Inuit to gather and stack rocks - eight to ten feet tall - in a cold and harsh environment? Why create solitary figures where few will ever see them? There is no practical reason, no political purpose, for the *inuksuk*. But when walking alone on the icy tundra the shapes bring the solitary man the comfort of company. An illusion of not being alone.

I walk about the storage room. Off the shelves and balanced before me are the pieces Jack thinks are most worthy: six fired terra-cotta, three bronzes, a couple of reliefs, some painted plasters, and two tombstones which had been rejected by mourning relatives because they were too ornate, too extravagant. As I look over the collection I add in my mind the pieces that wait at home: *Three Figures*, the *Satyr and Nymph, Mutual Boredom*. And of course the star of it all next door. *The Imaga Dea*.

I heave a large unfinished wax out of my way. It is crated, packed with polystyrene and supported with a wire armature. I can almost see inside the box. I'm sure that the wax is damaged by now. Without opening it, I know that I would never be able to repair, finish and bronze it in time. Let alone afford the casting. Standing at over 6 feet tall, the head would cost well over five thousand to cast. And wax does not show well. It looks unfinished.

I reach behind the box. My fingers touch something. A small piece. It feels painted. I have no idea what it is until I recover it from the dark corners and bring it to light. It is small, crudely painted and childish. My first real piece at school. A marble. Her forehead is high and intelligent, her lips

are generous and amused, her eyes are deep set and nostalgic. I
run my fingers over every feature. Why did I paint over this
and hide the stone? What was I hiding from myself? My
thumb rubs hard over the eyelid trying to pry away colour. But
I already know what is below the vividly crude shades. Sorrow.
The piece was a study of sorrow. I painted bright colours over
my mother's face to hide a truth I didn't want to witness.

I miss her. I do not miss my mother when I am defeated,
sad or lonely even. I miss her when I succeed. When I create
an object of beauty she will never see, when I have a show she
will never attend. I miss her in times of accomplishment,
when I imagine she might feel a sense of pride. Pride, and a
knowing that her sacrifice was not in vain.

"Are you okay?" A man's voice behind me. Jack. He is
already clean and presentable for his date.

"Yeah, I'm fine. Why?"

"You look sad."

"Do I ? Sorry." I wipe my nose over my sleeve.

Jack crouches in front of me. Reaches into my lap and
takes the image of my mother from me. He looks at her for
what seems a long time, turning the small bust over in his
hands. Then he places it amongst the chosen pieces.

"It needs to be refinished. The painting is crude. But below
that the work is fine and delicate."

"It's an early piece. I can't refinish it, you know that. The
marble was porous. The paint has soaked into the stone. It'll
always look crude."

"Cast it then. You'd lose this one in the process but..."

"No. I don't want to cast it. Just put it over there with the
rejects."

I nod toward the corner of the storage room where
everything second rate rests. Jack moves it to the shelves on

the other side of the room. His back is toward me. I can faintly see the movement of his muscles as his lifts her and places her safely with the others. He turns to leave the storage room. His body speaks of the extra hours he's taken on in my absence.

"Jack?"

He pauses at the doorway. The sun hits him in such a way that all expression is shadowed. He is the dark outline of a man. Any man. Any young man. Jack's body is supple. His movements have a fluidity that belie the aches that come from stone-cutting. One hand slides down the doorframe. The other still grips the wood above his head. From his fingers, along the stretch of his arm to his body is a limber line that takes the eye over his ribs and taut waist, down his narrowing hips, along the expanse of his legs until the interruption of his boots. As if he reads my thoughts, he leans a bit closer, into the room. He is suspended by the strength of his grip. His are young hands. Strong hands. Hands that grasp and don't let go. He leans. I see his face, his eyes, his expression. Bemused.

"What?" he asks.

I hesitate, then, "How long do you think you can stand like that?"

Jack drops his arm. Cracks his neck. "Forget it. I'll never pose for you again."

I meant to tell him how I know I've been selfish with our friendship. How I rely on him. And that I've taken advantage by cutting hours so that I could prepare for my show. But when my eye is captured, I am without words. Sometimes I am without sense. Of course I've noticed Jack's physical qualities before. But I haven't paused on them, haven't lingered for too long. I've never looked at him as though he were a stranger.

Jack puts his hand out to me. I reach out for him and he lifts me to my feet. I smack the dust off the seat of my jeans. And although the reject shelf is behind me, I can feel the painted gaze of my mother watching me.

"Come on. Let me help you sort through this stuff. Then I gotta go. Why don't you stay here and start sanding your piece."

*****

The Imaga Dea awaits my touch. There will be no cold exteriors for her. A sharp drop in temperature will crack her, destroy her. She is destined for an interior life. A life of comfort, so unlike the brave inuksuk of the north.

I run my thumb over the sandpaper, feel its subtly abrasive grain. I start on her backside, a broad surface that can handle looser strokes. My hand circles, as though I had a bath sponge and was enjoying the pleasure of washing Premika's back. Softly, now. Mustn't scratch her. Mustn't lose the texture of the clay.

How could she ever be copied? She could be nothing but clay. Not steel, not bronze, not a logo for a company. Premika's desire to manufacture her, to mass produce her is ludicrous! There can only be one *Imaga Dea*.

There are many *Davids*. Copies everywhere. The three *Davids*, however, are full-sized. A trinity of male perfection. *David* the bronze. *David* the plaster. And *David* the holy marble. *Blanc* marble. Carrara marble, carried down from the Italian mountains. The whitest of white marble. Pure and hard and cold and remote.

Once upon a time, the original *David* - the only *David* then - stood as symbol of Florence within the city square. Country wives brought their daughters on the eve of their weddings to stare at *David's* naked and relaxed body. "This is what a man looks like. Do not be surprised tomorrow night." And the country girls weren't surprised, just disappointed.

David has a beautiful, although a somewhat small, penis. Even flaccid, his penis is a lovely shape. Perfect really. Not a single impure thought could be had staring at that noble face, that sinewy marble body, that exquisite and delicate penis. Delicate compared to those large, defined hands. Strong, muscular, chiseled hands. Hands potentially dangerous to his delicateness.

Michelangelo and, much later, Rodin chiseled overly large, detailed hands. They exaggerated them. Why, when there are many equally beautiful body parts? I believe that it is because of the relationship every sculptor has with his hands. No matter how rough or dry they may be, if the hands are prominent in the work then the sculptor, too, is prominent. Hands are the sculptor's tool. And mine, although apparently as rough as a man's, leave an imprint on my work. Just as Michelangelo left the mark of his hands on *David*'s perfect body.

In this light *The Imaga Dea* is more than lovely. The restless fingers of Apollo have stretched across the sky with indolent nonchalance and, seeing her, have reached through Jack's floor to ceiling windows to touch the clay flesh of my making, turning her earthen body a rosy shade. Perhaps the gods do visit me from time to time.

I pick up a soft, human hair brush. I run the silky strands over her warming body. This I understand. This is real to me. Tangible, immortal, and constant. The human hair gently casts off a few grains of fine but impertinent dust from my gentle sanding.

"There," I tell her. "You're perfect now, as perfect as *The David*."

*****

I prepared for my first solo exhibition, busying myself with details and decisions. I catalogued my work and carefully chose the pieces. I sent invitations to architectural firms and galleries. I moved ahead hoping and assuming that Boris would okay my pieces. He told me to worry about the work while he worried about the artist's statement.

"A manifesto is only important if the art can't speak for itself."

"Oh Alex, it's not that your art can't speak for itself. It's just that the downward spiral of the voyeur's imagination has interrupted the conversation between them, the public, and you, the artist. Trust me."

"I think you said that to me once before."

"Yes and it paid off didn't it?"

"No, I still don't know what you mean."

And so I left the words to Boris while I concentrated on the visuals and tried to imagine ways to pay for it all. There weren't enough hours in the day. Twice, I had to put Premika off, and she seemed to resent it. She couldn't believe I was making plans without her, didn't think me capable. I finally agreed to a quick lunch, during the work week, on a day Amadeo said it wasn't too busy. If I was going to make the time to see her, I wanted to be sure that I wouldn't have to share her with Victor.

*****

I wait for her in front of the Art Gallery of Ontario. Seat myself upon the large, overbearing Henry Moore. It is developing a fine patina. The process has been hurried along by the many school children who slide along its feminine curves and climb inside its massive, solid body. Hard as they have tried, neither parents nor officials can keep the children from touching, climbing, sliding. It seems they have finally given up and the children have become a part of the installation. But is the structure sculpture?

There is an old story about "The Girls," Francis Loring and Florence Wylie. Two of the founders of the Sculpture Society of Canada, and visionaries in their own right, they were often completely broke and desperate to make a sale or win a commission. After a long cold winter together in their unheated old church where they worked and lived, it looked like Florence, the smaller and feistier of the two, was about to be commissioned by a well heeled Toronto couple. Wanting to impress, the wife announced that she was quite a collector and even owned a Henry Moore. Florence wasn't impressed. The couple were asked to leave the premises and Florence refused to sculpt for them.

'Why did you do that?' Inquired a hungry and cold Francis. 'We need that commission!'

'Anyone who owns a Henry Moore cannot appreciate sculpture,' retorted the outraged Florence.

I place my hands firmly on either side of my seated bottom. Touch the bronze and feel a warmth where the sun has stroked the surface before me. In ten or twenty years time this mellowing patina will take on a smooth, slightly different colored, surface to the rest of the sculpture. It will have an added depth and an almost buttery texture. This is a piece that will age well. A piece, unlike *The Imaga Dea*, that is meant to be exposed to the elements, the wind, the snow, the summer heat and the sweat from thousands of tiny playful palms. How could Florence hate Henry so much?

Like me, Florence and Francis were figurative artists, although they were somewhat more prudish in their content. Abstraction was something they too easily shrugged off. I have often done the same with my contemporaries. Suspicious that they hide their lack of talent and technique inside the doctrines of the abstract movement. But just look at this monster of a piece my bottom rests on! It begs you walk around it, consider it. The shapes are alluring, sensual. Touchable.

Perhaps it was easy for Florence to dismiss Moore's work because she never saw it in context. In a field, surrounded by sheep, the Henry Moore becomes organic and part of the landscape. Not a modern work at all, but something as pagan as Stonehenge, as honest as the inuksuks up north and as primitive as a Haida totem. In an urban setting, the Henry Moore seems out of place until children climb upon it and play King, or sometimes Queen, of the castle.

"Sorry I'm late."

Premika is bare faced, unadorned. She apologizes for her appearance, says it's because she's so busy. She runs a hand through her hair, smoothes it, then twists it off her face. She seems skittish, jumpy from lack of sleep. Raw and unmasked.

"Late night?"

"No more," she sighs, "those days are gone."

We make our way down along Dundas to Beverly then up to the rows of restaurants along Baldwin. I feel like some pesto pizza at John's Italian Café, but Premika is tired of garlic. She shrugs at the suggestion for something savory and opts for sweet and French. She opens her large purse, a soft suede creation in a golden caramel tone. Out come swatches of fabric and wallpaper for their condo's decor. I flip through them, feign interest.

"Favoring earth tones these days?"

She shrugs. Doesn't really care about the swatches either. She glances at a menu, runs her finger along the entries, purses her lips in a slight pout.

"You haven't asked about my wedding plans."

"You haven't asked about my exhibition."

"*Touché*," she replies.

"So? How are the wedding plans?"

"Fine. We are going to go to Montreal first. Have a little family thing and then on to Bombay for the wedding."

"Oh," I say. "And am I invited?"

"Well, you're not quite family and I doubt you could afford the ticket to India."

"I see."

The plates arrive, but I have lost my appetite. I cut my crepe into bits and push them about my plate with my fork. Separate the filling from the pancake part. Line the pieces of fruit along the edge. Put the mixture into order.

"Is it what you really want?"

She shrugs.

"Why do it, only to divorce later?"

"It'll work."

"Do you love him?"

"Stop being so cynical."

There is no point in arguing. Premika has once again reinvented her life, moved on.

*****

I'm not sure why my lunch with Premika left me with a feeling of discontent. I knew if I let my guard down, I would open the door, invite depression in for a visit. Then that dark blanket would wrap around me and prevent me from work. I would snuggle down into its alluring folds and forget everything. Purpose, deadlines, and self.

Artists are vulnerable to fits of depression. Most of us have little money; depression is one of the few luxuries we can afford. The suffering poet. The melancholic painter. The introspective artist of every variety. There are benefits to an artist's depression. It can, when it's not debilitating, be quite inspiring. The world lets you down and you go into your studio in order to create a better world. You shake a fist at God and yell at the top of your lungs, "I can do better!"

There is, for many of us, a prolific period before the depression completely settles in. It is called *hypermania*. Van Gogh produced the majority of his work in the final twenty-nine months of his sad life. Cesar Pavese produced two full novels in the two years preceding his suicide, then left behind a note which read, "*Not words. An act. I'll never write again.*"

The suicide rate amongst artists is as much as seven times that of the general public. It is true that the arts attract a less than stable spirit to them. But I prefer to believe that the artist, like the lover, is blessed with divine madness. An ivy clad Dionysus dances wild and drunk, tormented and blissfully ecstatic. Swinging between the two worlds, he is friend to both artist and madman alike. Twice born, of god and mortal, he is earth and divinity in one. And to be touched, to exist on both planes, *is* madness. It tears the soul in two directions, desiring both the comfort of humanity and the ecstasy of the gods.

Art is the impossible connector between two worlds. It says to mortals, 'Look, we're the same. I'm alive. I can be as tangible as you because I, too, can create on a physical plane.' But it is a deception because the creation is almost always useless. It is no more than a corporeal metaphor for what is divine in the human soul. And so we fool happier beings with our manic work, and the schism between what is real and what is perceived as real increases.

I chose to go to work at Milestone Memorials for the remainder of the day. It was strange to go back to my day job, after listening to Premika's plans. But part of me needed it. I needed the stable company of Jack and Amadeo. They grounded me.

"You came back in the nick of time," Amadeo said to me, "I was about to replace you."

"You couldn't replace me," I joked back.

"You're right. I couldn't find anyone who agreed to come in late, drink all my coffee and flirt with Jack."

"I don't flirt with Jack," I protested.

"Naw. I'm just an old man. My eyesight is going."

"Can I ask you something?"

Amadeo sighed. He could never say no because as much as he wants me to finish the day's work, he is always ready to converse and give his opinions.

"Do you think I am cynical?" I asked him, believing that he was the one person who would answer the question the way I hoped.

"Of course you are. But if you scratch a cynic hard enough, you're sure to find the heart of a romantic. They are the two sides of the same coin."

He put me straight to work on a pinkish-grey slab of granite. And as I traced Jack's stencil on the stone, as I started to cut and grind, I planned my show in my head.

*****

Pygmalion picks up a chisel, moves toward Galatea, wanting an excuse to touch her, to make himself felt. He moves in closer. She is perfect, complete, the ultimate woman created in the image of Aphrodite herself. To strike another blow, to alter her in any way, would destroy her consummate beauty. He puts the chisel down. At some point the artist has to know when to stop. When the work has reached an apex and another touch, even the slightest rubbing of fine sandpaper, is too much.

I put the sandpaper down. Boris will be here soon and there is nothing more to do. The time has come to stop.

The Heart Desires. The Hand Refrains. The Godhead Fires. The Soul Attains.

So often the stages of death are cited. Denial, rage, self pity, grief, acceptance... But what of the stages of creation? In his Pygmalion series, Sir Edward Burne-Jones painted a poetically grave young man in love with his own creation. A creation that had four distinct stages.

The Heart Desires shows Pygmalion looking at the image he is creating. He is, perhaps, more beautiful than the statue; this would explain why he has rejected all mortal women. And so he sets out to create something more wonderful, more perfect than the gender he has come to despise.

The Hand Refrains shows Pygmalion with Galatea, the stunning creation of white ivory. He holds his chisel, wanting to leave his mark on her creamy-white body. To make her feel something, anything, even the force of his hand. But the hand knows better than the heart. Pygmalion puts the chisel down.

The Godhead Fires is Aphrodite's response to his plea for a requited love. Not wanting him herself, the ever astute goddess breathes life into the ivory.

The Soul Attains shows Galatea, now flesh and blood, filled with adoration for her maker. The cold, unresponsive stone is now warm and yielding. The impenetrable white is now flushed with the embarrassed blush of a virgin's want.

These are the four stages of creation. The best of us can only presume the first two. It is hubris to fall in love with your own creation. Hubris to pray that your creation should love you in return. Hubris is punished by the gods. Pygmalion's woman must have been superlative. Must have pleased the gods. Must have appealed to Aphrodite's vanity.

What will the gods think of *The Imaga Dea*? What will the mortal Boris think?

I would not turn her to flesh, even if I could. Why would I wish death on something I love? Pygmalion never loved Galatea; he only desired her. He took an object of worship and made her mortal, simply so that he could possess her. A sculpture as lovely as the goddess of love, as lifelike as a woman, forever denied to us by a man's sexual desire. Poor Galatea! Created to be adored, but fated to suffer childbirth, grow old and die like any common woman. The story has been immortalized. But not the work, not the statue, not the art.

Boris arrives. He's never been to the storage space I share with Jack. He has also never stepped foot inside my apartment with its sloping ceilings and claustrophobic rooms. I always went to him. I suppose I never wanted him in my everyday life.

He seems quite comfortable here. There is no snobbishness. Only the judgement of my work. He's already familiar with many of the smaller pieces, but the larger ones are just too heavy to bring to him. No point in moving them before he okayed them. So I stand here and await his verdict. *The Imaga Dea* is covered with a sheet. She mustn't overwhelm the other entries.

"You're agreeing to cast the *Three Figures*?"

"Yes. It's at the foundry."

"Good."

No point in telling him that I can't afford to get it back from the foundry. There are still six weeks. I may yet find a way to pay for the casting without relying on Boris.

"I thought you weren't keen on that piece. You said it was a vanity piece, remember?"

"It is a vanity piece. All your work is vanity. But at least in bronze one can admire your virtuosity."

"But it doesn't fit your mandate if it doesn't say something... Perhaps it won't work with the other pieces."

He puts his hand up. Hushes me. "Be thankful, Alex, that I'm giving you a show. Don't ask for my approval as well."

He walks about. He's aware of the large shape beneath the sheet. Knows I'll show it to him, but has the grace to wait. He pauses before a small, male torso. An early piece, actually carved in marble, sculpted before I had the sense to be overwhelmed by the medium. Before I became superstitious about marble. Boris doesn't remember it. He touches it, feels its masculine lines. He's impressed and tries to hide the fact.

"Some girls keep diaries with locks and keys. Some men have the proverbial notches on their belts. You make sculpture," he laughs. "I suppose that wouldn't be a very good manifesto though."

"No."

Mutual Boredom sits cheekily on a shelf. It is still wax, so unlikely that it will be in the show. I feel a desire to laugh while I wait for Boris to notice it. I was complimentary but the figure of him looks more bored than George Sanders' voice ever sounded. Boris smirks at the sight.

"Okay. We can bronze that one. Not overly flattering of me but, once again, Premika is divine. Not sure if it is your show or Premika's at this point!"

He stops before the sheeted, life-size figure. The time has come. If Boris can't see the merit of *The Imaga Dea* then all our planning and all our work will come to an abrupt stop.

"Now, what have you been hiding from me?"

"It is my answer to you about mandates and the usefulness of art."

I lift the bottom of her sheet. Boris lifts an eyebrow.

"I suppose you've turned the tables. A female artist, objectifying the woman the way we men have objectified women for centuries. Makes a feminist statement, I suppose."

I slowly pull at the sheet. It falls away from her body, cascades over the clay flesh and pools around her feet in soft, discarded folds. Boris sees her for the very first time. She saves her most disdainfully haughty and superior look for him. I step away, let him get close. He just stares at her.

"Well?" I ask.

He turns on the spot, takes an abrupt step towards me. His arm raises. His hand follows. He's going to strike me. Mark me as Michelangelo was marked. But then the hand that offered to pay to cast my work remains generous. He touches my cheek, lifts my chin. Looks me in the eye for what seems a very long time. Then, deliberately and clearly he says, "Well done, Miss Hoff. You win. Well done."

****

"You're fired!"

Jack and I stare at Amadeo in disbelief. But he isn't looking at either of us. He is looking at *The Imaga Dea*. Does he mean that Jack has fired the terra cotta or that I no longer have a job? I wait, expecting some clarification but none is forthcoming.

"Well let's crate her up and get her on the truck," he says.

Boris had offered to pay for a moving truck to transport the work to his gallery but I declined. I knew that I would need him to pay for the casting of three pieces. I didn't want to owe him too much, be too indebted. As it was I would have to sell at least three of the smaller pieces to repay him. And so it was decided that Jack and Amadeo would move *The Imaga Dea* with the company truck.

Jack starts to prepare the packaging. The bags of styrofoam chips and the wraps. He does this quietly, ritualistically. He looks like a nervous lover wanting, yet unsure how, to please.

"How long have you worked for me?"

"Couple of years."

"Good. You can get unemployment then."

"Really? You're letting me go? Really?"

Amadeo helps lift the sculpture. Carries it with Jack to its wooden crate. Only now do I realize how like a coffin it is. They lay her down gently. Cover her in chips.

"You waste your time working for me."

"But, I need to work. I need a job."

Amadeo shakes his large head. Squats beside the crate and touches her face, before reaching for the cover.

"Don't be silly. Don't let your job get in the way of your work. Do what you are meant to do. You will find the means to survive."

There was no arguing with Amadeo. He was right. I would have to make a success of it. There was no net to catch me now.

CHAPTER 10

The subways have slowed; it is past rush hour. Not many on the platform. Everyone has gone home to have a life with family, friends or lovers. Not me, I stand waiting for my southbound train, determined to board the next one regardless of its colour. Premika would be more particular. Always waiting for the red. The red rocket.

I have noticed that people have started to call the Queen Streetcar the red rocket as well. It isn't the red rocket. The Gloucester trains, the red subways imported from England, are the only red rockets. Must be awfully expensive to ship them from England; they are so much weightier, more substantial than the silver ones made in Quebec.

I have learned to tell the colour even before the train arrives. I can hear the weight on the tracks. I can tell by the slowing of the train. They sound different, the reds and the silvers. Today I do not have to break my custom. I hear the grinding, the screech and the tired huffing of an old, heavy red train.

*****

I recognize Jack from a block away. He's leaning against the gallery wall, blocking the sign that bears my name. His arms are crossed, his body easy and relaxed, his eyes are half-closed and bored. I'm surprised at how much happier I suddenly feel.

"Jack! What are you doing here?"

"Waiting for you, what do you think?"

"Well why don't you go inside?"

"I can't stand Boris. Smug bastard."

I peer through the window. Boris has his new assistant with him. A young woman in a mid-thigh suede skirt, cowboy boots and a loose white shirt. A more recent student than me perhaps?

"I brought you a present. It's in the truck."

"I really should go in. You can come with me. I mean, you transported most of my stuff for chrissake."

"Maybe later," he says, making a move away from the wall, "come see your present."

I follow along, down the side-street, eager to know what he thinks of each piece now that they are properly displayed. I can trust Jack. He would be honest.

"Do you think the show will be a success?"

"Well there were a lot of stickers on the pieces."

"No," I tell him, "they're there to create a buzz, apparently. That's what she's for." I nod my head toward the younger woman beyond the window.

Jack raises his eyebrows in that questioning way of his. And so I tell him how Boris had, just two days before, asked her to place red dots on many of my pieces. He had a handful of them, both full and half-dots.

"So did someone preview your work?" he asks me, aware that the full dot means a sale while the half suggests serious consideration or an offer.

"No, I don't think so. When I asked him what he was doing he shrugged me off as though I were a nuisance. That's when he said something about creating a buzz."

"Stupid prig. You don't need that, your work speaks for itself."

"You think so?"

Because Jack takes my work abilities for granted, he assumes that I do as well. He doesn't, and couldn't, know how fragile my ego is. Large and breakable. It could shatter with a disapproving glance from anyone worthy of a comment.

"You know, that piece, the woman you're in love with? She looks fuckin' great in there. She doesn't need a dot. She's a great work of art."

"She's my greatest work of art."

"No," he corrects me, "you haven't made your greatest piece yet. You can't rest on your accomplishments. She may be your greatest piece so far but, if you think she's always going to be your greatest piece, you might as well kill yourself right now."

"That's a bit harsh, isn't it?" I laugh.

Jack pulls the gate open on the back of his pickup. With a leap he's in the back and reaching a hand out to me to climb aboard as well. I hike my skirt up to my thighs and steady myself in my one inch heels before putting my hand into his calloused paw. With a strong and steady yank I'm hauled up. My foot hits something hard, hidden beneath a tarp.

"I get the feeling that this isn't a bouquet of roses."

"Nope. I'm not a flower kind of guy." He crouches beside me on his haunches. "I hope you like it. That it doesn't offend you."

Jack reaches under the tarp and drags out the package. It is wrapped up in newspaper and bubble wrap but he has tied it up with a red ribbon. I pull away paper and protective coverings.

"You might find a place for her in there," he says, nodding toward the gallery.

The last bit of plastic frees her. I turn her over, see her face. She's free of garish paint and childish colours. Only a slightest trace of the hues I had used to conceal what I could not face. She is muted, quiet and loving. Her almond eyes now seem accepting; her lips are now forgiving.

"Jack..."

"I hope you don't mind."

"Thank you."

"Thought she should make it to your first show, you know."

"Thank you."

I lean over to thank him, to kiss his cheek, but somehow he turns his head accidentally and my mouth grazes his. We both pull away, panicked.

"I'd better go in. Boris is..."

"Yeah. You better."

"You're not coming in?"

"Naw. It's not my world in there. That world is closed to me," he says, each word a cautious step toward some explanation. "I haven't the talent or the ambition. That's your world now. I don't have the heart for it."

"It's not my world. My whole world is in my studio."

"Naw, it's in your head actually. You have an interior life that would confuse most people."

I open and stretch my fingers, so that he can slip his between mine. Hand holding. That is what I need now. But not even Jack will be able to do that opening night.

"Does it confuse you? My inner world?"

"I don't know," he laughs, "I haven't been inside you."

Jack helps me down, places the marble into my outstretched arms.

"Can you manage it?"

"I'm stronger than I look."

"I know."

"I can't believe you did this. How did you manage it?"

"I put in a lot of extra hours. Remember?"

I take a breath, ready myself to re-enter the world of Boris. He won't want to add this piece but I'll stand my ground. My mother will be at my opening after all.

*****

"There seem to be more and more silver trains. Do you think they are phasing out the red ones?" I ask Boris as soon as I enter.

"I hadn't thought about it really."

Boris is having the walls of the gallery repainted. A warm white. Something elegant but understated. Clean.

"You know that Premika only takes the train on the North-South Line."

"Is that so?" he asks. Could he sound more bored?

"The tracks are different. They only run silver trains east-west."

"I hadn't noticed."

"What? Your Mercedes never breaks down?"

"Wealth is the trait you most hate in others." He could be right. He often was. I hated that about him. He motions for his assistant, opens his wallet and hands her fifty dollars. Sends her off to buy us all lunch.

"She won't be at the opening, you know."

"Who?"

"Premika."

Boris laughs.

"What's so funny?"

"It isn't about her, it's about you. It's your show. When are you going to get that through your head? It doesn't matter how many pieces look like her. It is your show."

He puts his arm around me and ushers me through the gallery, wanting my opinion on details. Details that I have no opinion about. All I know is that she told me that my opening conflicts with her Montreal trip and I know, I know, that she wants to attend my opening about as much as she wants me to attend her wedding. Here the paths diverge.

*****

Premika's sitting on the stoop when I get home. Her knees are gathered up and her head's resting against them. What is she doing here in the middle of the afternoon?

"What's wrong?" I ask.

"Everything. Everything is wrong."

"Come on. Let's go in."

I take her upstairs, into my bare studio. No *Imaga Dea* to comfort her, no *Three Figures* to amuse her. No *Mutual Boredom* to surprise her. Only me. How much easier it is to deal with her when I have backup. A familiar face to turn to, a solid figure to support me. I could always turn to them whenever she left me speechless.

"I went to see Boris," she explains. "A few days ago. I thought if I spoke to him, without you there, I might talk some sense into him."

"Oh, Boris has sense," I say.

"He doesn't have *business* sense. He's supposed to represent you and encourage sales. Besides, when did you become so fond of Boris?"

I shrug. Why upset her more by saying that the enemy of my enemy is my friend? Boris may have once been the enemy, but he has redeemed himself. Compared to Victor's crass materialism, Boris's pretentiousness is a breath of fresh air.

"So what happened?"

"He said that someone else wanted to buy *The Imaga Dea* and he doubted that Victor would pay what she was worth."

I sigh. It was silly. Boris knew I had no intention of selling her to Victor and, as far as I knew, no-one had made an offer on her.

"You know, there was a time I would have just given her to you, if you had just asked. But I can't sell her to Victor. It's enough that he has completely possessed you." Honesty is a risk but now I feel there is no longer anything left to lose so I let her know how I feel to have lost her. Why I cannot give her what she wants anymore.

"Then sell it to me. I'm the one who wants it. The only reason *he* wants it is for *me*."

"Premika," I use her name gently. The name that means lover and racehorse combined. "Why? Why do you want it? You've never been a collector. Not of things, not of art, not of people."

Premika stops crying. The tears vanish as easily as they had run down her cheeks just seconds ago. Yes, she is a consummate actress after all. Victor is right to put her in his films. But one day, one day, she'll get tired of putting on her public face. She'll get tired of playing a role. The curtain will rise and she won't step onto the stage.

"I'd rather look at her than look in a mirror. She's a better reflection of me. Nicer maybe. She isn't as superficial as I am."

Oh if I could hold a mirror up to her so that she could see more than those nascent lines which are starting to etch the map of her life into the vulnerable surface of her skin. If I dared to hold the mirror of truth to her face, what would she see? The very thing she sees when she looks at *The Imaga Dea*. But the image of truth can hold you, trap you, until the most loving voice is no more than a faint echo.

"Premika?" I whisper.

"Hmm?"

"I don't know what I should do. I really don't want to let him have her."

Premika stands, brushes the front of her trousers as if to rid herself of my dust. Any trace of my surroundings, any marks or fingerprints, are smoothed away.

"It would be easier if you liked him a little," she says, now composed and in control of herself.

"It would be easier if he were a little likable."

She goes to the door. But instead of leaving, she latches the chain and turns. She is watching me. Saying nothing. But the way she leans against the door frame, the way she holds her gaze, the way she waits, says everything. *I could be yours if you would just play along.*

I know I am being played. I know this means nothing to her. But to me, to me, it means everything. One step and her fate is sealed. One step and I lose. One step and I have a moment only. A moment that will leave me feeling more alone than if I do not move at all. But that moment, that moment right now, is everything.

"I don't think I can do it."

"Do what?" I inch forward just a bit.

"I don't think I can marry him."

"No?"

"No. And now he's talking about living most of the time in India. He said he has a beautiful place in Goa. He thinks I will like it there. On the water."

Her hand has slipped between the silk of her shirt and the warmth of her skin. I can see her fingers through the folds of the material. They are stroking her belly. Small, tight circles.

"I told my mom about you," she surprises me.

"What did she say?" I ask.

"She asked whether I was sure about my marriage. Said it sounded like I was in love with you."

"Are you? In love with me?"

"Yes. I think I am."

Another step closer and I will be able to smell her perfume. And if I reach out my arm I could almost touch her.

"You think you love me?"

"I know I do. That's why I didn't tell Victor about us. He could never make me feel the way you do. I know that now. I would give up my career, my future, everything, if I could just change things, be with you instead."

Wasn't she the one who said it was time to put away childish things? Didn't she say that the mundane would destroy us?

"And do what?" I ask her. "Get a part time job waitressing?"

Premika may not desire Victor but she needs him. He will assure her future. Make her a star of his films, give her babies, provide for her. He will have her throw parties for his colleagues and show her off at film festivals. He will keep her in the public eye. Alive. What could I do but love her?

"I just want you to love me again. The way you used to."

And the distance between us lessens. My hand reaches into the tangles of her hair. I yank her face closer to mine. I want to consume this woman. Have her inside me, live in me. So that no matter where she is, I can be her home.

"Marry Victor," I tell her, "but keep me as your lover."

*****

I am much better at starting, than completing. With a new idea there is an upsurge of energy, a dose of inspiration. A high. And then a nascent beginning full of potential and promise. But as the shape takes a form of its own, the promise makes way for reality, completion. An unfinished piece isn't a piece at all. It is an attempt. I am a successful artist. I have a solo show coming up. My studio and storage space are filled with finished work. But I am also a failed artist because I believe my work is incomplete. Because I am an attempter, I continue to live.

Victor phoned. Seemingly out of the blue. Asked if I had considered his offer to buy the piece. *The Imaga Dea*, did he mean? *That* piece? I didn't bring up the wedding. I just told him that my head wasn't wrapped around the idea of a sale just yet as my show wasn't quite up and running.

Then, a few nights later, he appears, like a nightmare, without warning. No apologies for waking me. As if stopping by after midnight was quite normal.

"Something wrong?" My head between the door and frame.

"No, the contrary I'd say." He waits for the door to fly open.

"Victor, I'm sleeping."

"Got a little business opportunity for you. Let me in would you?"

He gets straight to the point without foreplay or fuss. No flirtation or talking in circles. I could admire him for that.

"Look, I want to be fair. I know you're fond of it. It's your best work from what I understand. So you tell me, what's it worth to you?"

It is his first time in my apartment. The space seems too small to contain him, the slope of the ceilings not bothering to clear his head. He has to stoop as he passes by me. Bow his head.

"She's priceless," I look at my clock, hoping he would notice the gesture.

"Well, maybe I can help you price her," he deliberately ignores my gesture. Victor isn't in a hurry. He isn't tired. He's the sleepless hunter, the restless competitor, the deal maker.

"Why do you want her? It makes no sense. Not as an investment, surely. There's been no estimate," I lie. Boris had suggested a price.

He changes tactics. Appeals to my sentimentality. Says he would give the sculpture to Premika on their wedding night. I just sit there, silently waiting, hoping Victor will get bored.

"If I set a price, a high price, that will set the standard for you. Don't you understand how it works? You're only worth what someone is willing to pay. I'm actually helping you."

"I didn't ask for help, Victor."

"Look," he continues, "if I pay you, say, ten thousand dollars then that's your worth. Ten thousand dollars. But if I inflate that price..."

"She's worth much more than ten thousand dollars," I cut him off.

"Well of course, it's hypothetical. We haven't established her price yet, right? And I'm willing to provide you with an inflated price-tag which will inflate the price of everything you sell from now on. It will set a new standard for you. My extra few thousand will translate into an extra few thousand on every piece you can unload. It's business."

"And all this time I thought you were motivated by love," my voice is too tired to carry the sarcasm. Victor takes my words at face value.

"I am. But not my own. I do not love the piece. I could have anyone in India make a clay sculpture for a lot less. There are many good artists there. Excellent ones who would make an equally good piece for a lot less money. It is for Premika. She loves it. Think about it." He pauses, but not quite long enough. "It could be from both of us."

He stares at his feet. Italian leather, burgundy with tassels. Did he slip them on, then slip out the door? Or was I his last stop on his way home to her? And when I lift my eyes, I catch his directly. Not cold, not intense, not penetrating. They're just eyes. Not even monster eyes. Just eyes.

"You know, it would be a lot easier for Premika if we got along better. You are her best friend and it tears her apart that we do not get on better. Do you hate me so much?"

I could answer him, tell him, "Yes. I hate what you represent. The purchasing class. A class whose whims dictate my very survival because your money can buy me." The truth is that I should love the Victors of the world because their wealth allows me to work, to live, to eat. But with the generosity of dispensed wealth, the purchasing class acquires not only the art but the artist as well. The Victors of the world pay the artist in order to possess the art. With Premika it is different. She also pays the artist but does so with her time and beauty so that the art can possess her.

"It's for Premika. A gift, that's all. To make her happy." He gets up to go. Very erect, very sure of himself. A winner. "Don't answer yet, think about it. And if you find clean hard cash vile, imagine owning that painting you loved so much. It's all up to you."

"That painting isn't worth anything and we both know it."

The moment of truth. Victor laughs with the sound of someone who has been found out but doesn't care. It's the 'well you can't blame a guy for trying' sound that women know too well.

"Well, I thought the painting spoke to you. Had sentimental value." He reaches into his inner pocket, takes out a long envelope and places it on the table.

"I know you can't make it to the family service in Montreal, so I took the liberty of buying you a ticket to India for the wedding there. It will be a big party, very fancy. You will be an honored guest. Let's try to get along. Okay?"

The temptation is too great. As soon as he's out the door I open the envelope. An airplane ticket. An itinerary. And folded in the piece of paper, a signed cheque. Fifty-five thousand dollars. Holy fuck!

*****

Premika called to say that she was off to Montreal the next day. She enthused about me coming to India. I could leave that Saturday evening, right after my interviews. She would be on the same plane out of Montreal. But, unlike me, she would be in first class.

"You know he's spoken with my father! Just wait till he sees me. I'm going to be hennaed from my fingers to my shoulders and I'll be in a red jeweled sari..."

I made love to this woman only a few days ago, believing she was mine. But Victor has ultimately won. I offered her love, immortality and a moment frozen in time; he offered her both her past and her future. A lost father, returned. The babies she hasn't met yet. He offered her something tangible and everyday. And sweetened it all with pomp and circumstance and a film career. How could I have ever competed with that? Victor was the victor. I could only hope that she would keep our bargain.

"You're going to miss my show."

"I know, but I did see Boris the other day and he showed me everything as he was preparing the gallery. It looks great. You will do fine."

"Not the same thing," I say.

"No," she breathed, "nothing is the same anymore. Will I see you there? At the service, in India?"

What to say now? After intimacies and desire, after obsession and creation, what is left? Polite conversation that ignores what once existed? I see divorced couples who, sharing children, keep it all polite and nice for the kids' sake. A discussion about holidays or the change of the weather. Keep it all on the surface because underneath is the truth. And the truth is that there was once fucking and fighting. That mouths once explored every inch of a body. Shared saliva and sweat. The truth is that not only the flesh was penetrated but the souls and the hearts of what once were lovers. And then all that remains are polite individuals pretending to be amicable friends. I cannot hate anyone I have been intimate with, but I can resent the tearing away, the wound that is left when the tearing apart is over. A wound that never heals but cannot kill.

CHAPTER 11

There are ghost trains in Toronto. Empty cars rushing through the tunnels barely slowing at the stops. Speeding. Going nowhere. I wait. Alone on the platform. My damp evening clothes wrapping around me.

I must enjoy this time, savor this moment because my life will never taste the same again. I have unveiled her. Laid her bare to the world and, in doing so, have laid myself bare as well. No more being that artist hiding behind the image of an unseen sculptor. Now it is up to the world to decide who and what I am. I will be under the scrutiny of the public eye. If I can hold the gaze a while, then I will have a standard to maintain. Her standard.

Of course there were other pieces at my showing. Strategically placed, one leading up to the next. It was a planned path leading to where she finally waited, a warm light bathing her naked pride. There she was, unashamed of her incomprehensible beauty. A stretching body. Beyond movement and limitation. Reaching, reaching, past the crowd to infinity.

I watched amongst the crowd. Critics, collectors and fashionable others. It amazed me to see them all there. Wanna-be artists and see-and-be-seen types. Of course, no-one recognized me. No-one knew that I was the name on the folder. I was just another face lost in the crowd. A stranger looking in. My showing was an excuse for these people to get out and socialize. To eat and drink for free. I had done the same a number of times. A new gallery opens, an artist shows his or her work, and no matter how inspired or uninspired the event, I was always consoled by the idea of limitless hors d'oeuvres. Why should my opening be any different?

No-one paid attention to me. I was invisible. Able to catch the buzz. Listen in without notice. Hear the sound-bites, then move on.

"The brie cheese is very good, try it."

"I'm opening in a play next month."

"Is there any more wine?"

"She's not still seeing him, is she? Doesn't she know?"

The gossip seemed endless. The idle chatter. But then I was inexplicably drawn to her. She seemed to call me over in a whisper and so I approached her hesitantly. I expelled the expectation on my breath as I blended spy-like. Under that one light the mundane slipped away, if only for an instant before their glasses were drained. Before the reality of a necessary refill. And so I inconspicuously drained my glass as well. And I listened.

"She's remarkable, her body seems more alive than someone living."

"Thank you." I acknowledged, though barely audible to the very eccentric old hipster.

"Why are you thanking me, young lady? You're not the artist?"

"I am. And also the server it would seem. Would you like a refill?"

The woman laughed and grabbed my hand. Then she called out that a toast was in order. I must have blushed as she insisted, raising her glass, "A toast to the last living classicist." I'm sure she meant *neoclassicist*, but I didn't correct her. I let her propose a toast to me. I'm sure she could have drained the glass, had it been full. The party chatter stopped because she repeatedly banged her fork on her glass, grabbing everybody's attention, if only for a moment. Then, embarrassed, they applauded politely so that they could resume whatever talk was most important to them.

But some stayed in front of her. Speculating about the model. Imagining our relationship. And whispering about her body. The more they spoke of her, the more they set me apart. I thought this would be my night but I couldn't enjoy it.

A slap of sudden cold air snaps me back to the present, to the empty subway station and the sound of wind within the dark tunnel. How easy it would be to step too close. To fall onto the tracks and into the tunnel where surely a train would soon emerge.

At the end of the evening I chose to walk for hours. I walked along the sidewalks, taking no notice of traffic, streetcars or buildings. I continued along Bathurst St., past the old church that now serves as a theatre. I turned my back on the Vegas-style lights of Honest Ed's and headed along Bloor Street. Walking at a pace until the traffic lights stopped me.

A small bird lay dead at the curb. Cars passed by without notice. But when the onslaught of traffic eased another bird flew down to its broken body, fluttering and chirping in a panicked dance. Cars came, and the bird flew away. But once they passed, he flew down again, only to resume his charade. As if to say, '*Get up, get up! Its too dangerous here. Don't you see, stupid? Get up. Don't just lie there.*'

"She's gone. She's left you forever," I told the bird, "it's best you fly away."

But the bird didn't believe me, didn't give up hope. He persisted to the point of his own exhaustion.

"Go on home," I said as I picked up his mate and moved her away from the road and placed her inside a planter. The bird remained. I walked away. Now, somehow, the bird and the rain seemed far more real to me than my show's opening.

As the first streaks of grey coloured the morning sky, I stole away to the closest subway station to board the first train of the new day.

But it is a ghost train, empty. "OUT OF SERVICE" boldly written across its forehead.

The morning papers will be coming out now. In my mind there are reviews about me in the art section. I imagine a new life opening up for me. A life I have dreamed of. But a life without the constant presence of my muse. I'm at the edge now, suspended between the new life and the old. Dangling, dangling. Hanging by a thread.

A hanged man will often orgasm at the point of asphyxiation, his semen sinking into the ground below. Such a man was considered "well hanged." Centuries ago in Britain, the country folk believed that a love root would grow there and whosoever ate together of the root would forever be bound in love and desire. The dead man, a sacrifice for eternal passion. Sacrifice. What could I possibly sacrifice to ensure love?

My first real opening. My first solo show. It seemed a great success. I was well received. Applauded, even. And yet I feel empty inside. Let down somehow. Like a kid looking forward to Christmas and then it's all over and so disappointing.

As a child, achievement was always rewarded. If I was first in my class my parents took notice. The rewards were affection and praise. I was the only one who existed in their eyes. I was alive and real for them because I had achieved. Every year I would set out to maintain my standard. I would work and struggle so as not to slip, so that at the end of the year they would notice me once again.

I still expect some kind of reward for my accomplishments and so I feel ripped off now. Disappointed. Disappointed because Premika wasn't there.

Another gust of air. A red subway train to carry me home. Home to bed. Home to sleep. In the lonely embrace of an empty bed.

*****

I look at my progeny. Not a child of bone and blood beneath the flesh, but a surrogate child of fired clay. Of all my pieces I have loved her best. Am I capable of letting her go?

"Love is a strange thing," says Boris. "Most of us project our desires and expectations onto those we fall in love with. Our lovers ultimately turn out to be less, or worse more, than our expectations. We're doomed. Love is fated to fail."

Boris locks the door, pulls the drapes. The gallery is closed for the night. He pours me a glass of his late vintage port. A secret stash he keeps under lock and key. Only twice have I had the pleasure of this liquid treasure. The first night Boris seduced me and the evening when my show was installed. Now, once again, I bring the rich drink to my lips and swallow. Sweet blood, warm and sticky. This is what should fill a communion chalice. Not some dry, thin red, but a hearty wine of substance.

"You're smarter than most lovers. You project your desires and fantasies onto your work instead. Premika may be less than you expected and hoped. But *she*," he gestures to my sculpture, "she is more."

"You're not making this any easier, Boris."

Boris fills his glass. He swirls the port around before raising it to his nose and breathing in its aroma. He has a very different enjoyment of the grape than Victor. Boris knows his wine by its taste, not by its label.

"What changed your mind? Why sell her?"

"She can't stay in my studio. She should be seen. Besides, I won't be able to work with her staring over my shoulder."

I can't tell Boris my real motivation. Parting with her is my sacrifice to love. If I send *The Imaga Dea* to their home in India then she will think of me when she is there without me. I cannot be with her always. And I cannot part with myself, cannot deny who I am, cannot forfeit the artist in me. The artist who is, who has to be, a selfish creature by nature. But if I can part with *The Imaga Dea*, I might atone for every selfish act I've committed against the ones I've ever loved.

I perch myself onto the edge of his desk. Slide my bum up, onto the fine old wood, between his scraps of paper and scribbled notes. His port is warming the lowest part of my stomach.

"I don't know," I sigh, "I'm enjoying my time off. It's almost a relief not to be consumed with an idea. To be like other people, you know? Pay my bills. Be normal."

"Well don't worry, something's bound to upset you sooner or later. At least, let's hope so, you're positively boring when you're like this."

The piece of happiness wedging its way into the disquiet of my life is the belief that Premika will return and be my lover. That it is me she loves. That no matter what happens, I will always have a part of her that belongs to me alone. My secret and forbidden lover. A perfect muse. I will work again when she returns. When we both return from this circus she calls her wedding.

"But why sell her to Victor?"

"Because Victor has given me this." I reach into my purse and hand Boris the cheque. His eyes widen when he sees the amount. "If I'm going to part with her, then I might as well make it worth my while."

"I'll cash this for you today. Just in case he changes his mind. Or you do for that matter. You're very clever. You get to gouge him and make her grateful in one grand gesture. Very clever. You've recovered well."

"What do you mean?"

"Well, in my experience no one ever fully recovers from love. I still miss my wife. I still miss you and I see way too much of you these days."

Boris looks self-satisfied. He refills my glass then pours a little more into his own. I slip myself off the desk and move away from the penetration of his stare. How can I be uncomfortable when I am surrounded by my own work? Boris moves behind me. Close like a shadow. He puts his arms around me and holds me with the awkward casualness that's reserved only for ex-lovers.

"I should have painted you instead of her, I might have done a better painting."

"Why didn't you? Paint me instead of her?"

He squeezes me. I cannot move, I am trapped in his embrace. He puts his mouth to my ear and whispers, "Because she was far more beautiful to look at than you."

I am free. He has loosened his grip and turned his attention to *The Imaga Dea*.

"You told Premika someone else was going to buy her. Was that just a way for you to get him to increase his price?"

"Not at all. I had a real punter. He's very disappointed."

"Really? Who?"

"Me. But Victor's offer is far more than I could have paid. Take it and get onto the next piece. Don't worry, he's just after the image. Eventually we'll offer to make him a bronze copy and your sculpture will be returned and put into a museum somewhere. He will get a huge tax write-off for it and your piece will end up where she belongs. Win, win all around."

*****

Saturday morning. 11 AM.

I sit amongst my pieces. I am being photographed as I talk about my inspirations, my influences, my process. Why are the questions always the same?

"So, who are your favourite artists?" he continues questioning me. He is Christian Hough, art critic for the Toronto Star. He is one of the critics that can change the life of an artist. He is tough, educated and discerning.

"To name a few is to insult the others." A side step. Familiar sounding. I wonder who used that convenient detour before me?

"But, surely, there've been influences?"

Oh that tiresome question! Every artist would like to believe herself an original. In solidarity with my peers I would have to respond, 'No-one. I am forging ahead on my own.' But in respect to those who have cut the trails before me, I would have to say, 'They all have. There is a long lineage and without them, there is no me. Every sculptor is an ancestor'

I know that neither answer would be satisfying to my interviewer. I suppose there's always Rodin with his substantial weight. Or Michelangelo with his figures partially emerging from rock, waiting to be liberated by the mercy of the stone cutter. But those answers are too obvious. These interviews require more obscure references. There are others who have affected me, moved me. I have wept over the beauty of Jean Baptiste Carpeaux's work. Clésinger's *Woman Bitten By Snake*, aroused me sexually even though she lay cold, stone dead. And Préault's bronze relief of a drowning *Ophelia* swept me away.

Made me dream of a world without question. A world without care. A world that has eluded me somehow.

"I don't know the name of the sculptor," I say. "He's unknown. And although I have been influenced by many works, I would not have become an artist if it hadn't been for *The Barberini Faun*."

"Oh God, here we go with that bloody faun again. Pretty soon she'll start telling you how she diddled herself over him," Boris pipes in. He stands to the side, arms crossed, overseeing everything. This is as much about pride for him as it is business. I am his discovery, his protégée. He needs me to do well.

I check my watch. 12:00.

Christian goes over to *The Imaga Dea*. He sees the full red dot.

"Want to tell me about this piece then?"

What to say? That Boris didn't rate me and so we made a bet. That it all backfired because I fell in love with my subject and she is, at this moment, marrying the man who's buying the piece. He is using my work to promote his company just as I used her beauty to promote my talent. Suddenly *The Imaga Dea* doesn't seem quite as beautiful to me, the conniving bitch.

"She has decided to sell *The Imaga Dea* for an unprecedented price. It will be an icon both in the west and the east. Her image will symbolize the beauty of film, an art form that makes all others obsolete. So although it seems that Alexandra has embraced a traditional expression she has also understood that every art form has a life span and, to extend that lifespan, to add a few years, one must view, and accept, the emergence of other art forms. The outstretched arms of *The Imaga Dea* are the arms of inclusion as she, the essence of sculpture, reaches toward the future."

Christian is scribbling. He's smiling. The review will be good. News will spread of the sale and I will be known. I have arrived and so I can do this. I can let her go.

****

Saturday, 4pm.

Boris has taken me to the airport. He has carried my bags in and waited while I checked in. I have gone through security. My bags have been searched, my body scanned. My flight goes to Montreal and from there on to Heathrow and then to India. I do not get off. The plane simply changes its flight number from 181 to 182.

Pre-boarding has started. First class and people traveling with small children. There are a couple of babies. A small toddler with green eyes and dark hair holds her mother's hand. She is so trusting and sweet. And just a little unsure.

"We will now start general boarding for flight 181 to Montreal, changing to flight 182, continuing on to Heathrow International before making its final stop at Sahar International Airport in Bombay..."

Premika must have looked like that little girl when she was a child. Wanting to be part of a bigger world, all the while clinging to her mother's arm. I saw a glimpse of that the first morning, that first morning she walked into my class. All bravado and vulnerability. I couldn't even draw her.

"Final Boarding call for flight 181..."

I look at my ticket, check the seat row. But even as I look I know that I won't be using it. I won't be on that flight. My impulse is to flee. How can I watch, how can I feign delight, as the woman I love says her vows to another. Till death they do part and all that. I do not have to go there. I do not have to witness their union. I have sent along my surrogate.

CHAPTER 12

I wait for a red subway. I stand behind the yellow safety-line, close to the mouth of the tunnel. Beyond the tunnel the tracks veer sharply to the right, beyond my field of vision. I won't know the colour of the train until it rushes from the tunnel and slows to its stop in front of me. Beat, beat, beat. My heart pounding in my constricted chest. Breathe, breathe. Just breathe. Maybe it is a mistake. Maybe they were on a different flight.

I first heard the news this morning when my morning alarm went off. Not the usual music to awaken me but a voice, a man's voice, a newsman. Breaking news... A terrible crash... Still unknown... A bomb... Irish air space...

At first I did not even register it. It was just soundbites. News. But then I heard the words "Air India Flight 182 from Montreal..."

I lay there, not believing, thinking that if I just change the radio station it will all be fine. It was a nasty joke. But every station, every newsman, was saying the same thing. A crash they all said. Air India. The flight went down in the early morning. The plane, exploded and split in half somewhere in the Atlantic.

I opened my mouth, gasped for the air that refused to fill my lungs. Not even the silence of my muted scream could dislodge the lump of culpability caught in my throat. Why, why, why?

And then the sound of a wounded animal as I struggled to inhale. I tried to steady myself. To hold onto something for support. But my studio was empty, there was nothing to catch me. I fell to the floor. On hands and knees. Gasping and retching in the guilty misery of my grief.

I should have called someone. But I just ran. I ran down the stairs and into the street. I just ran and ran and ran. I grabbed a stranger, asked him if it was true. He nodded and pulled away from me. Then, when I could run no more, I went underground, away from the perverse sunniness of this late June day.

*****

Boris opens his door to my banging. His eyes are puffy, nose is red and he looks wretched and pale. He stares at me in disbelief then grabs me and holds me close to his chest. Squeezes me. When he tries to speak, when he tries to say something, anything, only strange noises and breath can escape him. I feel his body shaking as he constricts me, holding me so tight and close that I can barely breathe. He fears if he lets go I won't exist. I am a dream, a spectre, back from the dead. But if he keeps me here in his arms, if he can hold me then he can reassure himself that I live. He thought I was lost, like Premika and *The Imaga Dea*.

"Thank God, thank God. Thank God." And he loosens his grip, takes my face into his hands and kisses my eyes and forehead.

It was only when I look at the spot where *The Imaga Dea* had stood only a day before that I go weak and crumple at the knees. I want to vomit. But there's nothing to wretch up. My belly's empty, as empty as my soul. Boris wraps me in blankets, serves me steamy cups of tea. But even as he comforts and cares for me, his grief continues to fall silently down his cheeks.

I don't cry that day. I hold onto my tears. I know if I cried I might lose a little of the grief that was now her. My tears can fill me. And as I absorb every drop and fill that unbearable emptiness, the abyss of my soul will have to increase in size to accommodate the pool of her memory. I hold on to my tears because if I cry there would be no end to them. I could never stop them up again. The flood gates would open and the tears would keep coming from a pool without boundaries. Salt water would stream down my face and soak my skin. Pour across the gallery floor and crash open the doors and windows carrying bits of wax and clay and bronze outside. Rivers would wash down the streets and the debris would carry stray children to the ocean where they would drown in my thoughts of her. No, I couldn't be responsible for that. I felt responsible for enough of it. I cannot, and will not, cry.

Boris finds a few cotton sheets. Drapes them over the *Three Figures* and *Mutual Boredom*.

"Just put them upstairs," I tell him. "No point having them on display."

"No point today," he replies. "Tomorrow they will do her honor though."

*****

I have no heart for anything. No voices in my ears, no visions in my head, only the sense of clay somewhere beyond the barrier I've built for myself with the shattered images of her.

I stare out the window trying to reassemble the pieces but I've never had a talent for jig-saw puzzles, only wax and stone and clay. Oh clay, so tangible and messy. But it doesn't move or breathe. Perhaps it never did after all. Perhaps it was not me but the muse who breathed the breath of life into my creations.

Boris has offered me another show. An attempt to coax me out of my miasma. He told me to use the sorrow. Told me to get on with life. Find some perspective. But perspective is a property of art, not life. Life is measured in increments of time. Validated by the fragments of memories. Fractured, each piece must somehow connect. But as hard as I try to piece it together, I see only a shattering of jagged images, not quite fitting, in the broken shards of reflection.

I stare out the window. I stare without the purpose of existence. I simply stare and try to place myself on that point on the horizon where everything meets. Infinity.

Far beyond the point on the horizon, somewhere in the heavens rests the constellation *Cela Sculptoris*; the Sculptor's Tool. If I slid the steel over my wrists to loosen the reins of my life, could I ride a celestial chariot and find myself resting there? Could I find my inspiration, the living breath of my muse, in the atmosphere of the Sculptor's Tool? *Ad astra per aspera.* To the stars through difficulties. I should be placed amongst the stars.

I cannot create or work. What use am I? What keeps me here? Not love. Not purpose. What? Why is it that I managed to trick Death when she didn't?

I imagine Death around me. Hovering. Pissed off that I tricked him. I try to push him from my mind, ignore the thought of him, but he stays with me. Watching me. Sometimes I think he's sitting in the corner, smoking a cigarette, or drinking a coffee, waiting, waiting.

If I let the thought of Death win, will I be reunited with her? Frozen, like statuary, in time. Never aging beyond the day we meet again as lovers? She promised me that. Promised to be my lover.

Lovers make vows to immortalize their love. They make a pact, forever and ever and evermore. There is no "Until death we do part," because the lovers' love is eternal. Greater than

Death and the ticking of time. Romeo and Juliet enter the world beyond together. Isolde follows Tristan to the grave. Antigone and Haemon, already entombed, embrace love and death as lovers do. To end life together is preferable to living life apart. And so ballad and tragedy, drama and opera, end with the lovers' death, again and again and again.

The suicide pact becomes art. In Japan, the suicide of lovers, *jyoshi shinju,* transcends birth right and class stratification as the unthinkable marriage becomes the eternal union. Puppet-masters and Kabuki actors dance to their glory, proclaiming the solution not only acceptable, but noble.

I make my decision. I go to the subway and listen for the train. I inch my toes closer and closer to the edge. I stand very close to the tunnel, waiting to feel its breath as it approaches. I see the telltale lights of an approaching train and its reflection hitting the cold, clean tiles. I hear the hard grinding sound, over the beat of my heart, as the train starts to slow, heavy and solid in its tracks. Red and glorious, fast and hard, emerging from the opening. It can be so simple. An end to pain. I can make it all stop. Make the hurt go away.

The screech of the brakes, a dull thump and blood. Blood all over.

But I do not jump. Death does not nudge me over the edge. I imagine it all in detail but I freeze. I cannot make that last move, cannot meet the train's force. I don't even get on it. I just walk back home. Defeated. Not a failed suicide. Not even an attempter. Just a woman, deaf to the sound of her inner voice. Lost.

I try, again, to throw myself into my work. Wedging clay. Paring away the excess. Paring away everything that isn't vital. Like memory. Escaping the past through the movement of my fingers. But they hold the memory of her. My fingers may knead the clay, they may separate the clay, they might even hold the clay but they are not able to create another work of art. They will not betray her.

Oh if God had only created a perfect world I would never have to dirty my hands with clay again!

*****

Jack has brought me back to work. Not because he thinks I would be of any use but because it is the only way he can keep an eye on me. After I told him about the day on the platform he no longer trusts me with myself.

"Amadeo wants to see you," he announces. And, unlike his usual self, he walks me to Amadeo's office and stands by the door. Amadeo's not alone. I see the back of a woman, sitting across from him. An espresso cup on the table before her.

"Ah Alex, we were just talking about you. This is Jean."

The woman turns in her chair to face me. She is a study in vulnerable bravado. A green, unfocused gaze. Dark hair curling away from slightly greying temples hovering above a strained and tired brow. Pale, pale beyond her colouring. A pale that is born of an experience beyond worldly comprehension.

"I found you," she says.

"Yes."

She has Premika's face. Her expression, her grace. She is an older Premika. A paler Premika. A Premika who managed to survive beyond the easy beauty of youth. Her hands are folded in her lap, her legs are gently crossed.

"You didn't come to the funeral."

"No," I say, "I couldn't."

"You didn't get to say good-bye then."

"No."

She sighs. A look of confusion interrupts the weary and worn expression on her face.

"It was just so arbitrary."

"Yes," I say, not knowing what I could possibly say to her.

I take a chair and sit next to her, but I cannot bring her any comfort. Cannot make gestures of empathy. There are no words to help her.

"I'm sorry," I say. I look away from her face, avoid her honest confusion. Our parents bring us into the world and it is our duty to see them to their deaths. When the order is reversed, when a parent buries a child, the world becomes perverse.

"They didn't find her body. So I can't bury her. There is nothing left of her. I didn't know what to do, so I went to that gallery and I met the owner. What is his name?"

"Boris," I offer.

"That's right. Boris. I was hoping to see that statue you did of her but he said that it went down in the crash as well."

"Yes," I say. "It was lost."

"But they found Victor's body. He was buried in Bombay two weeks ago. They were flying there to be united for life but ended up separated in death."

"Yes."

Amadeo clears his throat. It is only now that I remember that he too is in the room.

"Jean was thinking of a memorial. Something to remember her daughter. We thought maybe you could create it."

"I want a statue," Jean says.

"Yes," I say. It's all I can do. And the only way I can do it is to trust the memory of my fingers and to strike out against Death with the blow of my chisel.

*****

I approach the marble slowly. Irregular, pure and lovely. With just the slightest vein up the left side of it. This is what it has been waiting for then. I place the sharp end of the chisel against the smooth face of the stone. I lift my mallet, preparing for the first blow. *Strike clean and with intent. There is no room for mistakes.* The rage of the fire focusses my hand as it comes down to smite the marble, creating the first indelible mark.

I don't hear Jack come in. I'm not really aware he's stepped into the workroom. My intent is channelled, focussed on the stone. This is my way of mourning and remembering. She is contained in sensation and harbored by touch. Every trait, every feature, every gesture remains in the cellular memory of my flesh as I work.

"You've been at this for over three hours now."

I have lost track of time. All I know is that every blow is becoming more difficult. The muscles in my arms and back scream with each lift of my tools. My eyes itch and burn. My hands are raw and peels of skin are lifting in layers from the meat of my palms.

"You need to eat something,"

I glance at him for the first time. I sway in my boots and nod.

"Why don't you rest. I'll get you something to eat."

"No, I'll rest later."

The hammer comes down at a wrong angle, hitting the chisel awkwardly. I grab at the chisel, trying to right it. The edge catches my hand and rips into it, cleaving through the muscle and hitting bone.

"Fuck!" I scream out in pain. A fresh stream of blood pours onto the white stone. "Ah, fuck!"

Jack pulls the metal from my flesh. He makes me sit down as he cleans the wound. He wraps it in gauze and secures the dressing with gaffer's tape. Then he reaches for my chisel, but before I can say anything in protest, before I can yell at him to leave me alone and let me work, he places the chisel into my injured right hand, securely between my thumb and my bandaged mitt.

****

Her hands emerged first. One turns toward the viewer, open and resolved, the other turns inward, touching a space between the yet to be cut collar bone and breast. They rest at chest level. They do not reach from outstretched arms toward the heavens. No. They do not acknowledge an unseen god, only the unseen heart.

Next came the tangle of hair, and the angle of her head. A resolved face with full, quiet lips. *Not words, an act.* A raised, aloof chin. A chin of unknown determination. And eyes that are closed to this world. Eyes that look inward. Eyes that will never have to see disappointment or pain again. Eyes that no longer focus on the people who stand beyond her grasp. It is an enigmatic face. Sad and indifferent, this face holds a secret it will not tell. A knowledge it will not disclose. It is the face of Premika, the face that had slept upon my pillow. The face that scorned me and mocked me. The face that wept and declared her love.

I step away from the work. Wipe sweat from my face and pull the dust laden t-shirt from where it clings to my dampened body. The dust of her debris is already eating into my skin. Boring into my pores and scratching the surface of my sensitive flesh.

And my right hand pains me.

It's a Sunday. I'm here alone today. The stone is my focus for my sorrow and guilt. Only the sounds of a strike, a blow, a file interrupt the silence of my aloneness until a rap at the door breaks the rhythm of my work. I wipe the top layer of stone dust from my clothes as I weave my way to the door of the work area.

Her eyes settle on the marble. On a face, younger than hers but so much like hers. A quiet face. Premika's mother stands before the image of her dead daughter. Her hands trace the features of her daughter's face. A finger outlines the curve of her brow-bone, and runs along the contour of her cheeks.

"My girl. My girl. My baby." She touches the place where my blood stained the rock and rests her hand there. "I'm sorry. I'm sorry. I'm making a scene. "

"It's okay."

"Premika wasn't an easy child," she says quietly. "She was very demanding. Always had to be witnessed. She wouldn't even do her homework unless I sat there and watched her do it."

That Premika I knew. The Premika that had to be witnessed. Who needed adoration more than love and who, in the end, chose security and safety instead. And it killed her.

"Even while I was pregnant she was a challenge. I carried her high." She places her hand just under her breasts, "It was very uncomfortable and I was so young. But later all I could think was that I carried her closer to my heart than my two boys. Oh God, how could you let this happen?"

She looks at me. Looks at me through her tears and reaches a hand to my face. Wipes away a tear. Am I weeping? When did that happen? Streams down my face, cutting a clear path through the dust on my cheeks. These are not the pretty tears of sorrow. These are not the selfish tears of loss. No, these tears come from another place. Deep, deep inside the pool of my being. These are the tears of my whole lifetime, with all its memory, experience and regret. Tears for the woman here grieving her daughter. Tears for Premika and the love that might have been. And tears for the mother I lost before she would know me as a woman.

Jean gathers me up in her arms. Holds me to her tightly. Strokes the top of my head.

"There, there. Let it go, little one. God counts the tears of women."

I weep and weep and weep until there is no more. I have wept all the way to infinity, to that point on the horizon where all things meet. And I have found my way back, in the arms of the woman whose tears will never know an end.

"You've hurt your hand," she says, taking the bandaged mitt into hers.

"Yes."

"Is it hurt badly?"

"I think so."

"Has someone looked at it?"

"No."

"We'd better get you to a doctor then."

And I go with her. Not because I think I need a doctor, but because she needs to take me.

*****

Amadeo and Jack stand quietly. Their eyes fixed on me. I wipe my forehead with my unharmed hand. I'm burning. I know that my other hand, my bandaged hand, is infected but I don't mention this to Jack. I don't mention the antibiotics. I don't mention the trip to emergency or the look of concern on the doctor's face. I just stand with my two friends and look at her. She is done. The statue is finished.

"It's a great work," Jack whispers into my ear,

"I feel no victory."

Amadeo puts his arm around me. Takes me away from the workroom. He knows that I could strike one more blow, overwork the piece. He knows he will have to help me let her go.

"Come," he says. "We will have some coffee. And then we will arrange to send her to her new home."

Premika's mother plans to have her installed in a cemetery in Montreal. A family plot large enough that statuary is permitted. One day she, too, will be buried there, along with her sons, perhaps, and her husband. Until then, Premika's statue will stand sentinel. Waiting for the others to join her. Reminding them of the daughter who was lost in the sea.

She is a beautiful marble. Stone that is of the flesh. Hair that seems caught in the wind. Jack is right; she is my best work. A work of tenderness, beauty and love. In a few generations Premika will be forgotten. Her body a part of the waters that have taken her. And I will be no more than a name that is carried on the breath of the wind. Passing and ephemeral. But the statue will stay there, watching over the graveyard. The monument will remain beyond the memory of the woman who inspired it, or the memory of hands that created it.

Epilogue

They stopped running the red trains sometime in 1990. Each and every car, tired and retired, after over two million miles. They have all been replaced by the silver trains. Lighter, faster, sleeker and more efficient. More cost effective. More up to date. More uniform.

I no longer work for Amadeo at Milestone Memorials. The only itching I suffer comes from carving my own pieces in marble. Jack still, sometimes, finds me an incredible stone and calls me. But things have shifted there as well. He has become a partner in the business and has married Amadeo's daughter, Maria. I visit sometimes and drink Amadeo's coffee but this is becoming more and more infrequent. He has confided that he will retire, soon, after Maria and Jack have their first child.

Boris is showing my work again. I have been freed of fear and have devoted much of my time to marble. Bringing life into the stone and turning what is hard and stubborn into something as yielding and lively as flesh. The fire may not rage inside me with the same consuming intensity but, every time I reach for my chisel, I pick up the flaming torch carried and passed to me by those who came before. My work has matured along with me. It is weightier, more substantial and, from time to time, infused with political commentary. That said, Boris has taken to showing me even when the pieces have no value other than their beauty. *The Imaga Dea* changed him. She changed us both.

I live. I rarely feel the dark blanket wrapping around my soul. No longer keep company with Death. But something, I suppose, did die that day on the platform. Something in me escaped, leapt from my body and vanished with that departing red train. Left me behind, fighting to re-imagine my life. Leaving me to create another day without the romanticism and idealism of youth.

Sometimes I think about her, *The Imaga Dea*. I cannot help but wonder if she sleeps somewhere off the coast of Ireland, lost and forgotten, waiting, perhaps, for fishermen to drag her from the cold, dark waters.

It has been ten years. Ten years since Premika boarded flight 182 with Victor. Her body was never found. There are many questions. Many details still unknown. But I do not care why or how the explosion happened. I do not care that they are calling it the Air India *crash* when it was not a crash at all, but a deliberate act of mass murder. I only care that everything I loved went down with that plane. Went down in flames. And she was left there. Left like the *Inconnue*. Unclaimed and forgotten.

Sometimes Premika's image comes back to me, unasked. It seems anything can trigger it. A touch. A gesture. Laughter. A stranger's nuance. Sometimes no more than a scent. Hers. On the most unlikely people.

I'm following her scent. I trail it for blocks. And with every breath I almost see her. Almost believe she still lives. It was just a joke. There was no crash. But then the person turns a corner and crosses the street. Descends into the subway. Steals away her scent and she's gone.

She's gone. And yet my love for her remains, undiminished by time and death. Beyond logic and reason, love still exists. Love is not bound by the confines of society with its arbitrary rules. It does not define itself by age, gender or position. Love is an immortal spirit living in the temperate heart of the human soul. Unaware of time and borders, it is infinite. I have discovered infinity.

I'm waiting at the subway station. I'm waiting. But they don't run red trains anymore.

Acknowledgments

I am grateful to the following for their loyal support:

Daniel Matmor for his undying belief in me and for putting up with both the worst and the best of me on a daily basis.
Hal Eisen for reading far too many versions of this book and for his many years of friendship.
John Nobrega for the use of his amazing painting, *St. Lucy,* for my book cover and for so much insight into the world of art.
Aaron Brown, Sarah O'Sullivan, Alan Scarfe for proof reading.
Sonya Cote for encouraging me with great coffee and martinis.
Craig Sheffer for being my spiritual and creative mirror
Bob Blumer for his eternal optimism and help.
Matt Zimbel who convinced me that I was more than just an actor
Daniel Weinzweig for his encouragement and for introducing me to his mother Helen, who was my greatest writing mentor

I am grateful to **Cavanagh Lucia Matmor** for being as creative and smart as my protagonist. Without her I would never have made this happen. She makes me want to be a better person.

For Supporting Smart House Books I would like to thank:
Allan Eastman, Marion Lewis,
Gwynyth Walsh and Chris Britton,
Elizabeth (Libby) Lennie,
John Novak, Miriam Rottman,
Barbara March and Alan Scarfe,
Ellie Aylesworth and Martin Shaw,
Jody Glover, Kim Nelles,
James Kinnear, Steve Henderson,
Mark Kaczmarczyk, Colin Divine

I am also grateful for the support of
The Toronto Arts Council and The Ontario Arts Council